DASAINT ENTERTAINMENT
Presents

A Rose
Among Thorns

A Novel

by

Jimmy DaSaint

Copyright ©2011 by
DaSaint Entertainment

Written by Jimmy DaSaint

Published by DaSaint Entertainment

Cover design: beyondgrfx@yahoo.com

Printed in the United States

ISBN:
978-0-9823111-5-8

[1. Urban —— Fiction 2. Drama —— Fiction 3. New York ——Fiction]

Dedication

This book is dedicated to every woman who fell for the wrong man. And every man who caught her before she fell ...
—Jimmy DaSaint

Acknowledgement

First, I give all my thanks to my Lord Jesus Christ. You rescued me from darkness and showed me the light. Now I finally understand. To my Rose among thorns, Tammy "Boo" Mathis, my little sister. When everyone ran away, you ran towards me. I love you "Boo" more than any words I could ever write down on paper. To my mother Belinda Mathis, I love you mom for being you. To my brother Sean Mathis and sister's, Dawn and Tanya, thanks for all the support and love. When I come home it's on! To Marquise, Jeff, Nigel, I'm sorry for not being around to watch y'all grow. But when daddy returns I'll make up for every day, week, month, year, I missed. Special thanks to all of those who never stopped loving me. Valerie Henry, Anissa Phillips, Novaline Tanksley (thanks Nov, for everything) Dana Still, Yvonne Gray and the whole Gray family. Teri Woods, Karen Elmore, Ruby Lewis, Natalie Jackson, Shelia Ford, Elizabeth Newhart, Darrin "Jeek" Lockings, Maxwell Taylor, My two best friends, Robert Hennigan and Wallace "Duke" Gray, Rasi Baker, Mc-Breeze, George Dunbar, Tera Jones, Brenda L. Thomas, James Davis, Mr. Nate, Jerome Jones (Pitts). To all Mathis family. Mark, Mose, Eric, Larry, Candi, Vennessa, Bam, Jazz, Kyle, Sterling, Robin, Joyce, Annie, Gayle, Territta. Thanks to A&B distributors for giving me my first 2- book deal. Eric,

Wendy, Karen, Max Kwame. And a special thank you to my new book family- Amiaya Entertainment. Antoine "Inch" Thomas and Tania Nunez-Thomas. I'm here now, so let's get it cracking!   To all my homie's on lockdown, "Mo-Pointer (Detroit) Cornilious Kollock (N.Coralina) Anthony "Man" Durham, Roddell Smalls (Pitts) Bradley Hardy aka- Swift (Chicago) YG (Pitts) June (Trenton N.J) A.J. Blank (Michigan) Al-Money(Philly) Darnell Atchinson (D.C.) Elkton F.C.I. Schuylkill F.C.I. Allen wood camp, Low, F.C.I, Pen, Fort Dix, Fairton F.C.I, Camp, Lewisburg Pen, Camp, keep your head up to all my comrades in the feds and state prison system. (They locked us up; just don't let'em trap our mind) To my I.C.H-camp- Hands of stone. Sekue Clark, Cheeze, Dink, Colossus, Scarfo, Live, Corey, Shorty-Raw, Carlos, Pooch, Jeek, Razz, Stay strong y'all and stay focus. West, South, North, G-town, Mt. Erie, SouthWest Philly, 42nd St. 43rd, 52nd, 46th the "Bottom." 60th St. Wynnefield, 39th St. Camdem N.J- R.I.P. Harold "Georgie" Johnson, my I.C.H soldier I will never forget you homie. R.I.P also to Mark, Man, Troy, Rob, LiL Kenny, Ernie Floyd. May your souls rest with God for eternity?

A Word from the Author

This book is dedicated to all of the beautiful roses out there. The strong women who hold us down through thick and thin. Our mothers, wives, sister, aunts, nieces, girlfriends, mistresses and lovers. Women who step up and take charge when our backs are placed up against a hard wall. After I was sentenced to 10 years in federal prison I honestly had no clue of what was a head of me. Or who would remain by my side. Prison destroys alot of relationships and marriages. But prison is also a discovery of truth, love and loyalty. When a man or woman is sent away to serve time, the first thing that they will find out is who are their true loved ones. A prison bid will separate the fake from the real. Most people you thought cared, sometimes are the ones who actually loved you all along. It's God's way of clearing up our confused eyes. He put us all through certain tragedies so we can see then separate the real from the fake. Alot of people who I thought were friends are all of the people who wrote me letters and sent me cards. All of those who accepted my calls and told me to stay strong. The real friends know who they are. And all the fakes do too! They say, "Time heals all pain, and faith heals the rest." This prison experience has helped me so much. It helped open my eyes and give my heart to the people who truly deserve it. I was lost before coming to prison. But prison taught me the ultimate lesson. And the hardest lesson to learn. To love yourself. In the midst of all the drama I thank all of those who didn't run away from me in my time of need. May God continue to watch over y'all. And never, ever be a fake. Sincerely, James "Jimmy Da Saint " Mathis.

This poem is dedicated to every person on the street who lost a love one to prison.

"If prison takes me a way,"
By Jimmy DaSaint

If prison takes me away

If prison takes me away, would you run or would you stay?

Will our world continue to stay blue, or suddenly turn gray?

Will you at least come and visit, or write me once a week?

Or will you just forget about the magic nights we shared
between the sheets.

I know that you always tell me, you'll never leave me behind.

But if the cops come, and I lose everything, would you continue to stay by my side?

Would you forget about the happy times, and only remember the bad.

Start some phony arguments, to find a reason to be mad.

Would you ride like a true queen, and stay focused on our
plan?

Or talk about the women I sexed, just because you want
another man.

If prison takes me away would you disappear like all those
fake friends?

Do some things you would never do because you're running
low on ends.

Would you blame it all on me for leaving you?

Or would you pray that we both make it, and want me to
believe in you.

Would you forget about all the good sex, my warm tongue
tasting your soft neck?

The passionate love we made, our bodies covered in running
sweat.

See if prison takes me away, I'll miss that smile and those
   beautiful eyes.
 And pray to God to keep you strong. And don't turn you
    words to lies.
 See if prison takes me away. I hope things would stay the
    same.
I know you'll be hurt and missing me, but will you feel my
    pain?
See if prison takes me away, I'll think of you all the time.
And hope that when I return back home, that I can still call
    you mine.

> —Jimmy Dasaint
> The New #1 Author of street drama

A ROSE AMONG THORNS...

My black woman, my queen, I'm so sorry for what I've done. For taking you through these tragic times, with nowhere else to run. You are my strength, but I'm your weakness, breaking you by the day. Still you treat me like a king, loving me in every way. I owe my life to you, for saving me in times of need. It's only because of your love that I can still believe. I'm nothing without you, but with you I'm everything and more. Through this ghetto of weeds we live in, you remain my rose among thorns ...

By Jimmy DaSaint

Chapter One

Philadelphia, PA—April 14, 1998

The hard rain was falling like cats and dogs on this early Thursday morning as the group of people all stood around waiting for the bus to soon arrive. The 8:10 A.M. bus was usually on time when it would pick up these same individuals, every morning, on the corner of 45th and Market Street. But today, the early morning showers seemed to have slowed down the buses' regular schedule. As the people stood around waiting, a brand new white Infiniti Q45 pulled up. The driver rolled down the tinted black windows. "Hey, you gonna just stand there," the man yelled to a female that had been waiting for the bus to come.

"I'm with my girlfriend," she said, pointing at the girl who was holding the large umbrella over both of them.

"Both of y'all can come, hurry up," he said, unlocking his car door.

After closing the umbrella, the two women ran, getting inside the warm and dry Infiniti sports car. Once the red light turned green, the car slowly drove up the street.

"Hi Eric," the woman in the front passenger seat said.

"How you doing, Joyce? Are you going to work?" Eric said.

"I'm fine, and yes we're going to work," she said, smiling,

happy to be out of the pouring rain.

"Thank you, Eric, we surely would have been late this morning," she said.

"Where's your job?" Eric asked.

"Thirtieth Street, the Post Office. We both started last week."

"What do y'all do?" he asked, as he turned down the music that was playing.

"We separate mail in the mail room. It's a cool job. Seven dollars an hour ain't bad," Joyce said. "So I see you've been too busy to call me, Eric."

"Don't start, Joyce. I told you, you're like family, you're like a little sister."

"I'm 18 years old and I'll be 19 real soon. So how long are you going to keep calling me your little sister? You're only four years older than me."

"It's not about the age, Joyce. It's about the respect. My family and your family have been close ever since I could remember, ever since we lived in the projects, across the hall from each other."

"Okay, big brother, I get the message," she said smiling.

"Your girlfriend don't speak?" Eric asked.

"I'm sorry, my name is Rose," she said, looking out the window, enjoying the ride.

"She just moved around here. She lives on the 13th floor, in my building. We met at work and she told me that she lived in B-building, one floor above me," Joyce said, interrupting.

"Where are you from, Rose?" Eric asked.

"I'm from Cherry Hill, New Jersey," she said smiling.

"Oh, right across the bridge."

"Yeah, I'm a Jersey girl," she said, smiling.

"Oh yeah, well I'm a Philly boy," Eric said, looking at her through his rearview mirror. "You can't get no closer than that."

The rain started to slow down as it now was lightly drizzling. Pulling up in front of the U.S. Post Office on 30th and Market Street, Eric found an empty spot and parked his Infiniti.

"The Garden State, huh," Eric said, looking back at Rose.

"The City of Brotherly Love, huh," Rose said, smiling.

"Yeah, the City of Brotherly Love, and don't you forget it," Eric said smiling.

Rose said nothing as she and Joyce both smiled at the same time.

"Okay, ladies, y'all here on time," he said as the two of them got out of the car.

"Thank you, Eric, I mean 'big bro,'" Joyce said, being sarcastic.

"Thanks, Philly boy," Rose said, blushing, as she and Joyce walked inside the post office building.

After both women were safely inside, Eric pulled off and drove away.

"I think he likes you, Rose," Joyce said as they both took off their jackets.

"He's cute, but he's not my type."

"What! Eric is every woman's type, the nigga is fine, and he got plenty money," Joyce said. "What's your type?"

"I think he's cute, like I said, but I don't mess with drug dealers."

"How do you know he sells drugs?" Joyce asked shocked.

"I can tell. The way he talks, his clothes and jewelry, I can spot a drug dealer from a mile away. I got drug dealer vision," she said.

"Eric is a different type of drug dealer. He ain't running around faking like so many of these wannabees. He be trying to do big things. His family use to live across the hall from my family. They moved two years ago. Eric always was cool, always trying to help people. Once he started hustling, the first thing he did was move his mother and little brother out of the projects."

"That's nice, still a drug dealer is a drug dealer, and only pain and heartache comes with them. My father was a big time drug dealer in Camden, New Jersey. Now he's doing life in the feds. And my mother ain't been right since. I will not let myself go through what my mom went through, and still going through right now, not me, never," Rose said, looking at Joyce with a serious face.

After putting on their blue postal uniforms, they both clocked in and sat down.

"I'll just work my ass off and help out my mother and two little brothers. I don't plan on living in the projects all my life." Rose said.

"Well it's hard with no fathers around. Everybody's either dead or in jail, and ain't nothing left but the drug dealers. They're locking all the good men up. My father is locked up too, and it's been so hard without him around," Joyce said in a sad tone. "I'm most focused on helping my mom. I'm not even looking for a relationship."

"Niggaz is looking for women who needs them, then they'll treat us any kind of way. Trophey's! Then dump us when they find the next pretty face."

"My dad told me something one time and I've never forgot it. He said, *'Never let a man disrespect you. Never be nothing less than a queen, and never fall in love with a drug dealer.'*" Rose said.

Suddenly ...

A tall white woman walked up holding two large boxes of mail. "Here, Joyce," she said, passing one of the large boxes to her. "And this one is for you," she said, handing it to Rose. She then walked up the hall and disappeared.

"My son's father was a hustler," Joyce said, sorting the mail out.

"Where is he now?" Rose asked.

"Dead! Somebody shot him last year. Nineteen ninety-seven was a bad year. My father went to jail and my baby's father was killed a month later. Now it's just me, my son, my mother and two younger sisters. My mom is on welfare. My little sisters are seven and eight, both too young to know what's going on. And my baby is one year old. If I don't help my family, nobody will, and we can't always depend on Eric's couple of dollars," Joyce said.

"What!" Rose said. "What do you mean?"

"Sometimes Eric drops off a few hundred dollars to my mother, maybe once a week or every other week. Our mothers were real close. They both went to the same high school back in the day. He's been doing it ever since my father got locked up."

"That's a good man," Rose said.

"I told you that Eric was different. He has a good heart. I always had a crush on him, but he always looked at me as a little sister. Sometime I wish he didn't, but I respect that. A big brother is better than nothing."

"What's up with tonight? My mother said she will babysit. It's Thursday. I'm trying to go out to the club," Joyce said, changing the subject.

"Tonight, I can't. I got to go to my other job at my aunt's hair salon down South Philly."

"Do you ever get a day off? You work almost every night?"

"I got to. I got to get my mom out of those projects."

"You need a break, Rose. You're going to work yourself to death."

"If that's what it takes to help my family, then I'm going to

17

be one dead ass sister who died helping her family."

They both laughed as the two of them finished sorting the boxes of mail.

"If you go to the club tonight, maybe you'll meet Mr. Right, some hard-working 9 to 5 brother, with a Benz and benefits," Joyce said smiling. "You're an attractive woman. You can have any man you want."

"Thank you, Joyce, but I'm okay. I can't take off work, even if I wanted to. And I'm not looking for a man right now."

Rose was a very attractive woman with a honey brown complexion on her slim 5'7" frame, with long jet black hair, complimenting her exotic features. For all of her twenty years, men had always been attracted to Rose, offering to buy her jewelry, clothes, even cars. One time a man offered her a thousand dollars to have sex with him. She spit in his face and walked away. Never would she play herself for materialistic items, or money, for sex. Never would she let herself be treated less than a queen.

Joyce was also attractive, but she was the total opposite of Rose. With a body to die for, Joyce knew exactly what men wanted, and if the price was right, she would be all theirs. Her measurements were 36-26-38. Joyce was a redbone who stood 5'8" tall with long black hair laying down her back. When Joyce wasn't working, she was partying, or backstage up in some rap star's face, showing him why she should be in his next video.

Joyce had big plans and wasn't afraid to let anybody know. Her motto was:

"I lost my baby's father and my pop.
To survive, I can't stop.
Hustle to get that house and the 600 drop.
Even if I got to fuck my way to the top."

And she meant every word. She knew life was hard, and women in the projects had to work for everything they wanted, even harder than most women. The projects were full of girls like Joyce, pretty, uneducated females, with one or two children, waiting for prince charming to come take them away from this urban nightmare. With it rarely ever happening.

Chapter Two

The next day ... Friday morning, 7:58 a.m.

The sun was barely shining on this gloomy spring morning. Eric pulled up to the bus stop once again, like the day before. Rolling down his window, he yelled out. "Hi you doing *Jersey* girl? Where's Joyce?"

"She's off today. She didn't have to work," Rose said.

"Are you going to work?"

"Yeah, my bus is on its way. It will be here in 10 minutes."

"I can drop you off," Eric said.

"I'm fine. I don't mind catching the bus."

"I'm going that way. You could be there in 15 minutes," Eric said smiling.

Rose looked up the street. The bus would be on its way soon, but she could tell Eric wasn't going to take no for an answer.

"Okay," she said, opening the car door and getting inside. "I see y'all Philly boys are real persistent."

"Sometimes persistence pays off," Eric said in a smooth voice. "I was always told if you really want something, you got to work for it."

"It depends what you want, and what you work for. Sometimes you don't get what you want," Rose said.

Once the light turned green, Eric began driving down Market Street.

"So your boyfriend lives in Jersey?" Eric said, changing the subject.

"Why do you ask?"

"Oh, I'm sorry. I didn't mean to be nosey."

"Yes, you did, but I'll answer your question anyway. No, he don't live in Jersey."

"Oh, he lives in Philly?"

"No, he don't live in Philly either."

"New York?"

"No," Rose said.

"Where do he live?" A curious Eric wanted to know.

"I don't know 'cause I don't have a boyfriend," Rose said.

"A pretty girl like you, yeah right, you got somebody, somewhere."

"I don't choose to have a boyfriend. I got too many things on my mind right now. A boyfriend will be just another problem. Do you have a girlfriend?" Rose asked.

"I got friends," Eric said smiling.

"I didn't ask you that," Rose said.

"Well no, I just have associates."

"Oh, I get it," Rose said, folding her arms.

"Get what?"

"You got females who you can see when you want to."

"Something like that. What's wrong with it?"

"Better be careful. You can't keep an eye on all of them, playa," Rose said smiling. "Don't catch nothing you can't get rid of."

"Are you free tonight?" Eric said, changing the subject.

"Why playa? Looking for another *associate*?"

Eric smiled. "No, I don't need no more associates."

21

"Well, what do you need?"

"A time to pick you up."

"I'm sorry, cutie, but I got to work tonight."

"Do you want me to pick you up at work?"

"I'm fine, thank you anyway, but I'm really not interested in any new friends right now, *or* associates," Rose said.

Pulling up in front of the post office where Rose worked, Eric parked. Taking a card from his pocket, he passed it to her. "Here, pretty, just in case you change your mind. You never know, it might come in handy."

"I doubt it," she said, getting out of the car. "But, thanks for the ride."

"You're welcome," Eric said, staring at her beautiful face. "You're welcome. Think about it, you never know," Eric said, yelling out the window.

"Still being persistent, huh?" she said walking away.

"Always, when I think it's worth it."

"I like that, it's cute," she said, as she walked inside the post office building.

Once again, Eric pulled off and drove away.

Driving up Market Street, Eric's cell phone rang. "Hello," he answered.

"Yo, what's up E?"

"What's going on Mike? What's the deal homeboy?"

"Me and Larry is going to the strip club tonight. You down?"

"What time?"

"About 10 o'clock."

"Yeah, I'm with it. I have a few runs to make, but by 10 o'clock, I'll be ready," Eric said, pulling up to a Wendy's drive thru window.

"Okay. You can meet us at the crib, we can all roll out

together."

"I'll be there at ten with Braheem," Eric said.

"Okay E, I'll see y'all later dogg."

"Peace Mike," Eric said, closing his cell phone, as the young lady stood there waiting for him to order.

West Park Housing Projects, located on 46th and Market Street, in the Westside section of Philadelphia.

Three large high-rise buildings made up this small, poverty-stricken community. There was A building, B and C. Each building went to the 19th floor. The buildings were all old, built in the early 70s. Trash and beer bottles filled the filthy pissy halls. Graffitti was sprayed all over the walls and all on the elevators, consequently, out of order 90% of the time. But for so many less fortunate people, this was all they knew, this was home. And the West Park Housing Projects would have to do.

Outside the front of the buildings ...

Where children once roamed and played was now the home of drug dealers, crackheads and whinos. A modern day war zone. Even the police would stay away from this horrible place. A single, security guard would walk back and forth to each building, ignoring all of the crime that was going on around him. And he knew exactly what was going on, but he didn't care. A crap game on the 6th floor in A building, a number house on the 10th floor in B building, a drug house on the 15th floor in C building. Whatever illegal activity you could imagine, you could find it all at the West Park Housing Projects. Still, he never paid it any mind, and the people who lived there never paid him any mind. They knew he was just trying to do his eight hours, then go home to his wife and kids. And he knew that interfering in the wrong person's business could stop him from making it home to his family. So he didn't bother the people who lived here, and they didn't bother him.

The elevated train ran down the right side of the projects, on 45th Street. The buildings would all vibrate every time a train would pass by, usually every 15 minutes. Before the city gated off the whole area, young children from the projects would play on the train tracks and vandalize the property. A few years ago, a young boy was struck and killed by a passenger train while playing on the tracks. Ever since then, the city closed down the area, and barb-wired the gates to prevent kids from going there, but the barb-wired gates still didn't stop the tough ghetto kids from finding another way on the tracks.

Later that evening ...
Apartment 12-B ...

Joyce laid asleep on the couch, holding her son, Ryan, in her arms. After being out all night, she had just come in and decided to take a nap. Her mother was in her room with the door shut, while her two sisters, Aiesha and Brandy, were sitting at the kitchen table doing their homework. A hard knock at the door interrupted her peaceful nap.

"Who is it?" she said, laying her baby down and getting up to answer the door.

"It's me," a sweet voice said.

Joyce opened the door and Rose walked in. "What's up girl?" Joyce said, with her hair all over her face, and still wearing the same clothes from the night before.

"I just wanted to say hi before I go to my other job," Rose said. "I ain't see you since last night and today was your day off. I'm just making sure you all right."

"Girl, I'm fine. Joyce can handle herself. You ain't got to worry about me."

"So how was the club last night?"

"It was okay. I got a few numbers. I met a few ballers. I met some guy named Keith. He's from Germantown. Nigga got plenty of paper girl, I mean, a platinum Rolex watch, chain, and a platinum convertible CL 500 Mercedez Benz."

"I'm telling you, Rose, I could have fucked him all over those butter leather seats in that pretty ass car."

"No, you didn't," Rose said laughing.

"No, girl, we went to his apartment, the crib was fly too."

"Well, you must have enjoyed yourself. You stayed out all night."

"I got five words to say," Joyce said, tying her hair in a pony-tail.

"He was all of that?" Rose said interrupting.

"No. *Faster than a speeding bullet*," Joyce said, as they both burst out laughing. "He was fine too, with his tall chocolate self. I should have known it was too good to be true. I wasn't in his apartment for five minutes and he had my bra and thong off, I just knew this kitten was about to get tamed. All I can remember is he laying me down on the bed. Girl, I wrapped these thick long legs around his waist, and was ready to throw it on him."

"What happened?" Rose said, cracking up.

"He ain't get five good strokes before he was, *'oohh baby, oohh baby,'* then rolling over falling asleep. Tall, dark and use-less. After speedy was knocked out, I called another one of my friends on the phone and had some phone sex, playing with my pussy until I came. I was going to get my shit off, with him or without him."

"Girl, you is crazy."

"He ain't got to worry about getting this pussy no more. Well, maybe if he let me drive the Benz, I might change my mind," Joyce said, walking over to the couch laughing.

"I saw Eric today," Rose said.

"Oh, yeah? Where?"

"At the bus stop this morning, he dropped me off at work."

"You go girl. I told you he likes you."

"He was just so persistent, wouldn't accept 'no,' so I let him take me to work."

"Girl, you better jump on Eric. I'm telling you, ain't too many good brothers left out here on these streets, and Eric is all that."

"I told you, Joyce, I don't mess with drug dealers. I don't care how cute they are or how much money they got," Rose said.

"So you saying if Eric wasn't a drug dealer, you would let him take you out?"

"Maybe. I don't know. I'm still not looking for a relationship."

"I think you like him. Stop fooling yourself."

"I don't know him, nothing about him, how can I like what I don't know?"

"I do it, it's easy," Joyce said, laughing, "all the time."

"He gave me his card."

"Oh, he did?"

"Yeah, I still don't know why I took it."

"Don't be no fool and lose it, you never know."

"I'm positive, it could never be nothing between me and Eric. I know he got plenty of women chasing after him. I won't be one of them."

Looking at her watch, Rose noticed the time was getting late. "I got to get ready and go to work. I'll see you later, Joyce."

"All right Rose," Joyce said, laying back down on the couch next to her son.

Rose then walked out and shut the door behind her. After walking outside, a cab was out front waiting. Rose quickly got in and the cab pulled away.

Chapter Three

Later that night ...

Eric sat around with Mike and Braheem. A money machine was on the kitchen table, being used to count the weekly profits. Larry, another one of Eric's friends, stood by the window, making sure nothing suspicious was happening, as he looked through the curtains. The large 64" RCA T.V. was on in the living room. The guys had just finished playing John Madden Football, on Sony Playstation, now the game was playing itself. Eric dumped out a brown shopping bag full of big face hundred and fifty dollar bills. "Separate that, Braheem," he said, as he finished counting the money that was neatly stacked on the table in front of him.

"Fifty-six thousand. Business is getting slow," he said.

"How much is that Braheem?"

"Thirty G's," Braheem said, with three stacks, ten thousand each, now wrapped in rubberbands.

"All y'all take ten a piece," Eric said, getting up and putting the money machine back into the closet. "We're going to have to step it up fellas, the last three weeks we've been falling off. Mike, your strip only done $27,000, and Braheem, yours did $23,000. Larry out did both of y'all," he said, as he put the remaining $56,000 in a black Addidas sports bag. Each man picked up his stack of money, then they all walked back into the living room and sat down in front of the large T.V. screen.

Eric had known Mike ever since elementary school. They had both grown up in the West Park Housing Projects, and had been best friends since they both could remember. Mike's family had moved five years earlier to southwest Philly. But he and Eric maintained a strong friendship. A few years later, Eric moved his mother from out of the projects. A few blocks away from Mike. Many people thought Eric and Mike could pass for brothers. Both were 6 feet tall with dark brown skin complex- ions, only Mike had a small mustache. Eric was twenty-two years old, 170 pounds. Mike was twenty-one years old and ten pounds lighter.

Braheem was Eric's first cousin who lived in south Philly before he and Eric moved into their apartment eight months ago. Just seventeen years old, Braheem had been in and out of juvenile homes all his young life. Ever since his mother was raped and strangled by two men, after getting off work one night, Braheem had been a loose cannon, and Eric did his best to keep his younger cousin straight and on the right path. Braheem stood 5'8" with wavy hair and a light skin complex- ion. And everyone knew he had a very short fuse, ready to go off at any moment.

Larry was Eric's good friend from high school. They had known each other since being teammates on the school's bas- ketball team. Larry stood 6'1" tall, with a dark skin complex- ion. He had grown up a few blocks away from the projects, on 43rd and Powelton Avenue in west Philly. But now he was liv- ing in his own apartment in southwest Philadelphia.

Eric supplied each of these men with kilos of cocaine and pounds of marijuana. Mike ran a block on 53rd and Chester

Avenue in southwest Philly, while Larry had a 24 hour a day strip on 40th and Powelton, both distributing multiple pounds of kilos on a weekly basis. Braheem ran a drug house on the 15th floor in the C building of the West Park Projects, mainly used for selling marijuana. Each Monday, the four of them would all meet at the apartment known as the 'crib' located on 60th and Kingsessing Avenue in southwest Philly. This is where Eric would give out the weekly amount of drugs, count profits, and discuss business.

"What's up with the strip club, E?" Mike said.

"I'm still down, first I got to go put this money up then me and Braheem will meet up with y'all."

"We're going to the new club on 73rd and Passyunk Avenue," Larry said.

"What's wrong with the 'Ponytail'?" Eric asked.

"I'm tired of the same old chicks. That place is getting played out. We did that, time to move on. Plus I heard there's some fine ass honeys at this new spot. It supposed to be real classy, all types of women, white, black, Asian," Larry said.

"What's the name of the spot?" Eric asked.

"The Platinum Club," Mike said smiling.

"We'll be there," Eric said as the four of them walked out of the apartment and into the parking lot where their cars were all parked.

The parking lot could have been a scene for the Philadelphia car show. Eric's white Infiniti Q45 was parked next to Mike's 1997 cherry red Lexus coupe. Larry's 1998 smoke silver Mercedes Benz C-230 was parked a few feet away, next to Braheem's 1995 money green convertible BMW 325i. Each had a car in their favorite color.

"I'll meet y'all at the club in about an hour," Eric said, getting into his car. "Braheem, you follow me."

The men all got into their luxury sports cars and one at a time, each drove out of the parking lot.

Twenty minutes later ...

Eric and Braheem pulled up in front of the Korman Suites apartment complex where they lived. Getting out of his car, Braheem walked over to Eric, who had remained seated in his car listening to music. Eric rolled down the window and passed Braheem the black Addidas sports bag. "Put it up in the stash, put yours up too. I brought enough out for both of us to enjoy ourselves."

"Do you want me to put the burner up?" Braheem asked, patting his side.

"No, bring it. I never been to this spot before. Bring it just in case."

"I'll be right back," Braheem said, walking into the apartment complex.

A few moments later, Braheem walked back out and got into his car, then he and Eric both pulled off.

Thirty minutes later ...

Eric and Braheem pulled into the parking lot of the Platinum Club. The lot was packed with cars from front to back. Three beautiful women walked around in tight platinum cat suits giving out complimentary cigars. The Platinum Club was large. Word was that it was a front for the Italian mob. Outside, four big, strong, body-building looking guys were patting people down for weapons. "Do you got that burner on you?" Eric asked Braheem.

"No, I left it in the car."

"Cool, come on," he said, as they both walked to the front of the club.

"Step up," one of the large security guys said.

Eric and Braheem both stepped up. The man began patting them both down. "Okay, y'all can go in," he said, showing them the entrance.

Walking inside, they came to a window where a beautiful half-Asian and black woman was sitting. "Fifty dollars apiece," she said. "Do you have any I.D.?" she said looking at Eric through the thick piece of glass.

"Yes," Eric said, showing her his driver's license.

"And you?" she said, looking at Braheem.

Braheem pulled out a fake I.D. The photo was of his face, but the rest of the information described a white male, in his early thirties. Usually, no one ever paid it no mind, but she did, looking hard at the I.D.

"I'm sorry, you can't come in without proper identification," she said in a sweet voice.

Reaching into his pocket, Eric pulled out two big face hundred dollar bills. "Is this proper identification?" he asked, passing it through the hole in the window.

With a big smile on her face, she grabbed both bills, putting one in the cash register, and the other down her shirt. "Proper enough. That way," she said, pointing to another door.

Opening the door, Eric and Braheem's eyes both lit up from what they were seeing. Inside was the size of a grand ballroom. Over a hundred beautifully exotic women were walking around half dressed, in platinum thong sets. A male's paradise. The place was packed. It had to be at least a thousand men inside. Tables were decorated throughout the large room. A bar was on the opposite side, a few feet away from the large wooden stage. Three gorgeous women, one white, one black, and the other

32

Asian, were serving drinks to the group of men who were all half drunk and waiting. The Platinum Club was definitely the place to be. Eric spotted Mike and Larry sitting at a table, close to the stage. Walking over, he and Braheem sat down in the two empty seats.

"What's up, E?" Mike said with a beautiful gorgeous Tyra Banks look-a-like giving him a lap dance.

"You the man, Mike," he said, smiling at his friend.

"Yo, Eric, this is the hottest spot in the city, man. This place is off the hook," Larry said, unable to keep his eyes focused on one female at a time.

"I see, every woman in this spot is a dime-piece," Eric said.

Two beautiful women then walked up. "Are y'all okay? Do you need anything to drink?" one of them asked.

"Yeah, can you bring us two bottles of Crystal, and what do it cost for a lapdance?" Braheem said, as he couldn't take his eyes off the large breasts that both women were proudly displaying.

"Twenty dollars for ten minutes," one of them said.

"Okay," while pointing to the one whose breasts were a little bigger than the other's.

Relaxing in his chair, the large breasted, beautiful woman jumped on Braheem's lap and began riding him like a cowgirl at the rodeo, and he enjoyed every moment.

"They about to have a show in a few minutes," Larry said, yelling over the loud music.

"Yeah, some girls are going to come out and dance in a few minutes," Mike said as the young woman was getting off his lap.

"Here you go pretty," he said, passing her a hundred dollar bill and a card. "Don't forget to call me."

"Damn, Mike! How many lapdances did you pay for?" Eric

asked.

"Four, and I gave her a little twenty dollar tip. I had to stop, one more and I probably would have come in my pants," he said laughing.

"Here's your two bottles of Crystal," the young woman said, walking back to the table.

"How much is it?" Eric asked.

"It's $350 a bottle," she said.

"I'll pay for one," Larry said, pulling out a large stack of hundred dollar bills.

"Here you go pretty," Eric said, passing her his and Larry's money.

After whispering in the woman's ear, she got up off Braheem. "Okay, I'll be ready after work," she said smiling.

"Here Braheem," Eric said, passing him a stack of money.

"How much is this?"

"A G," Eric said.

"Cool, 'cause she bringing her girlfriend too," Braheem laughed.

"You need any help young buck? They some big girls," Larry said.

"No, I'm all right. I'm a big boy," he said, as everyone around the table started laughing.

"Destiny leaving with me," Mike said.

"Who?" Eric asked. "Who's Destiny?"

"Destiny the shorty who gave me the lapdance."

Walking over sitting on Larry's lap, a beautiful white woman began whispering in his ear. "Oh, yeah, I'm the special guy," Larry said, blushing.

"Yeah, just what Bunny needs, tall, dark and handsome," she said smiling.

"Well, what's up with those private rooms upstairs?" Larry

said.

"Fantasy, that's what's up. Where fantasies come true."

"What's included in a fantasy?"

"Everything. Would you like to find out?" she said, grabbing his hand.

"I'll see y'all later," Larry said, following the woman through the crowd and up the stairs.

"You the trick master," Eric yelled.

"Man, this place is making a killing, at least a few mil a week," Mike said looking around at all the people. The music was loudly playing Biggie's, "One More Chance,' as the large colorful lights were blinking on and off. Suddenly the song was turned down and a man walked out onto the stage holding a microphone in his hands.

"Gentlemen, we would like to thank everyone who came out tonight. I hope everyone is enjoying themselves with all the lovely ladies that's here."

The crowd began whistling and clapping.

"In a few minutes, we will have three gorgeous, very attractive women come out, one at a time, and perform for y'all. Don't be stingy, these girls will be worth every penny, as y'all will soon find out," the man said, walking back and forth across the stage. "The first is a beautiful young woman from New York City. Please give a warm hand for 'Heaven,'" he said, as the music was turned back up, and the gorgeous 'Heaven' walked out onto the stage in an angel outfit, with a halo on her head and wings on her back.

Heaven was 5'9" tall, with a coco brown complexion. As the music played, she slowly danced around the large stage. Taking off her wings and halo, her see-through thong set drove the men wild, as the roars from the crowd became louder.

Walking back to the table, Larry sat down. "Damn Larry!

That was only ten minutes," Braheem said laughing.

"That's all it took," he said smiling. "Fantasies don't take long."

After dancing to three songs, Heaven picked up all of her money that was on the stage and walked back behind the curtains. The men all clapped and whistled, all gathering around the front of the stage. The music was turned back down and the man walked back out with the microphone again.

"This is the only place in the world where y'all can find Heaven on Earth," he said, as everyone started laughing. "Next up is 'Fire: Please give a warm hand for this beauty coming all the way from Los Angeles, California, to our great City of Brotherly Love."

Once the music was turned back up, Fire walked out onto the stage. Dressed in a fireman's hat and coat, she flowed back and forth across the stage in her sexiest walk, hypnotizing the crowd. Taking off her jacket, her nude, 36-34-36 body finally was displayed, leaving the stunned crowd breathless. Fire stood 5'6" tall, with Asian features, and a long reddish ponytail going down her back. A tattoo by her navel read, *"If you can't take the heat, stay out of the kitchen."* And she was definitely the heat. The music played and the men paid, as Fire danced to the smooth Marvin Gaye song. *"Sexual Healing."* After dancing to Prince's *"Infatuation"* and *"Diamonds and Pearls,"* Fire collected all of her money and walked in the back to cheers and whistling.

A few minutes later ...

The music was turned down once again, and the man walked back out. "She can torch me anytime she wants," he said as the crowd again bust out laughing. "Next up, gentlemen, is a beautiful woman from Atlanta, Georgia. Please give a warm hand for 'Extacy,'" he said, walking off the stage. The lights were all cut off; only the spotlight remained on as it beamed down on the large stage. The sound of Luke's classic song *"I Wanna Rock,"* began playing from the loud speakers. Then Extacy walked out. Walking on stage in a maid outfit, the crowd went wild, as this beauty danced with grace to the hard hip hop song. Everyone went wild, throwing money all over the stage.

"Man, she is fine," Mike said.

"She is prettier than all of them," Larry said, throwing a hundred dollar bill on stage.

Eric just stood there, speechless, unable to believe his eyes.

Chapter Four

"Now that's what you call a dime," Braheem said.

Eric stopped two women who were walking by. "Excuse me," he said.

"Yes, cutie, what do you need?" one of them asked.

"I just want to ask y'all something," he said.

"What's that handsome?"

"The girl on stage," he said pointing.

"Who, Extacy? Forget about it. She ain't doing nothing. It don't matter how much, she dance, and that's it. No lap dance, no private rooms, nothing," one of the women said.

"Oh, really," Eric said with a smile on his face. "Any man who gets her is one lucky guy," she said. "Thank you," Eric said, giving each woman fifty dollars each. "Thank you very much," he said, watching Extacy do her thing on the stage.

"You're welcome. Anything else, *we* available," the women said smiling.

"No, I'm fine," Eric said blushing. "But thank you anyway."

"Hold up, ladies, one minute," Larry said, following them both through the crowd. Eric just remained stung, unable to take his eyes off Extacy.

Forty-five minutes later ...

After Extacy finished dancing, it was closing time. Everyone waited outside the front of the club.

"I'll see y'all tomorrow," Braheem said, walking toward his car where the two lovely females were both waiting.

"Yeah, E, I'll get at you too," Mike said, when Destiny walked out a door on the side of the club.

"What's up, E? Who you waiting for?" Larry said.

"Extacy! Extacy, that's who."

"Man, you heard what those girls said, she ain't doing nothing."

"I'll take my chances," Eric said smiling.

"What's up with you, Larry?"

"That's what's up," he said, pointing at an attractive white girl who walked out the side door. "Snow Bunny."

"I'll talk to you tomorrow, Eric, I'm out," Larry said walking towards the woman. "I'm going back to fantasy island," he said, smiling.

Eric walked to the side door and waited. One by one, beautiful women came out, each getting into different men's cars. After waiting for twenty minutes, Extacy finally walked out. "The cab will be here in ten minutes," a man said, closing the door behind her.

"Hi you doing, Rose?"

Turning around, she noticed Eric standing there leaning on the side of the building.

"How you doing, Eric," she said, shocked to see him standing there, outside of her job. "Was you inside?"

"Yeah, I was inside Extacy," he said, smiling.

"It's not what you think."

"You don't have to explain yourself to me, Rose. I don't judge a woman from what's outside, only from what's inside."

39

he said. "Do you need a ride home?"

"No, my cab will be here in a minute."

"Save your money. I can take you home. I took you to work," he said smiling.

"No, I'm okay, really, I'm fine, Eric. Thank you anyway."

"I'll just follow the cab and make sure you get home safe."

"No, you wouldn't."

"Yes, I will, right to your doorstep."

"Okay, Eric, you can take me home," she said. "You just have to be persistent, don't you?"

"Only if it's worth it," Eric said, smiling. The two of them walked back to Eric's car that was the only car still in the parking lot. After getting inside, he turned it on, and they drove off.

"I don't want you to think I'm some type of ho or something. I dance to help my family, and that's it," Rose said, rubbing her feet. "I don't leave with nobody or anything like that."

"You leaving with me. I can be some type of psycho or something."

"Joyce already told me about you."

"Oh, yeah?"

"Yeah."

"What did she say?"

"It don't matter, but it was all good."

Eric smiled and continued driving. "Are you hungry?"

"No, my feet are killing me. I'm going to soak my feet and go to bed."

"Can I ask you something serious, Rose?"

"It depends on what you want to ask, but go ahead."

"Why do you put up this hard image against me?"

"It's not just against you, it's for everybody."

"I feel like it's against me."

"Well maybe it is, I'm just very cautious."

"Cautious of what?"

"I been through so much the last few years. I had to drop out of college last year and start helping my mom out, and my family. If I don't do it, no one else will. I stay focused and cautious of everything and everyone."

"But all I want to do is take you out, maybe dinner or a movie."

"I don't have the time, even if I wanted to, Eric. I work at the post office, 8 to 4, Monday through Friday. Then I'm at the club every night except Sundays, my schedule is very hectic."

"What about Sunday?"

"I'm tired from working two jobs all week. All I do is go to church and come back home, getting myself ready for Monday morning. You're the only guy I met, since I moved here from Jersey a month ago. And I wasn't trying to meet nobody. Guys approach me all of the time, and I shoot all of them down. I really don't have the time."

Pulling up in the project's parking lot, Eric parked his car in front of B building where Rose lived. The moon was half full on this spring night. Only a few crackheads was still up on this early Saturday morning, as Rose and Eric sat in the car and continued talking.

"What college did you go to?"

"I was a sophomore at Temple. I studied Business Management and African Dance."

"What happened?"

"Things just got all messed up with my family, and I had to temporarily drop out because of financial problems, but it will get better, I just know it will. God is good. I'll be okay, me and my family will be all right."

"Do you have any brothers and sisters?"

41

"Two younger brothers, me and my mom. My father is in jail."

"When's he getting out?"

"He's not, he got life."

Opening the car door, Rose got out. "Thank you, Eric, for the ride," she said.

"Hold up. I'm a walk you upstairs."

"No, no, I'm fine," she said, showing him her can of mace that was attached to her keys inside her hand.

"I still have your card," she said, walking into the building.

After Rose was no longer in sight, Eric drove out of the parking lot and went home.

The next day...

It was Saturday, 10 a.m., when the phone rang. "Hello," Joyce said.

"What's up, Joyce?"

"Eric! What's up? I got the money you sent. Thank you."

"You're welcome. How's your mom and sisters doing?"

"Everybody is fine, Eric. They're still all asleep."

"Joyce, I wanted to ask you something."

"What Eric? What is it?"

"What's up with Rose? She cool, she's real serious, twenty years old, no kids, no man, why? I just wanted to know what was up, that's all."

"She definitely has a good head on her shoulders. I told her about you. I told her that you was a good man. She said you was cute too."

"Oh, yeah?"

"Yeah, but Eric, she ain't trying to get in no relationship, especially with a drug dealer, that's exactly what she told me."

"How do she know what I do?"

"Girlfriend is sharp, she just knew. Her father was a big time drug dealer over Camden. I think she's just scared of what happened to him and what her family is going through now. They moved from Cherry Hill, New Jersey, a nice neighborhood. I saw pictures of the house, a pretty white two-story home. I guess when her father got locked up, things fell apart, her family couldn't afford it anymore, 'cause she had to also drop out of Temple. All she talks about is getting her family out of the projects and staying away from drug dealers. She works two jobs, at the post office with me and at her aunt's hair salon in south Philly."

"That's what she told you?" Eric said.

"Yeah, that's what she said. She goes to church with her family every Sunday at St. Mary's Baptist on 34th and Walnut Street, and when she ain't working, she's in the house writing her poetry."

"She writes poetry?"

"Yeah, she's good too. She let me read a few. I think she like you for real."

"Why you say that?"

"I can tell, even if she denies it, she's just afraid of your occupation. You think she's cute, don't you?"

"Yeah, she's fine, I can't front, the girl is beautiful."

"Damn, Eric, you ain't never even say that to me."

"Girl, you know you fine. I ain't got to tell you, everybody else does."

"Thanks, Eric, I'll put in a good word again for you, but you have to do the rest on your own."

"Thanks little sis, I'll talk to you later," Eric said, hanging up the phone.

Turning on his T.V., Eric lay across his large king-size bed. The thought of Rose had stayed on his mind all night, in a way that no other woman had ever done before, and he had to find out why.

Chapter Five

Later that afternoon...

Sitting on the couch, the phone rang ... "Hello," Rose said, answering. After a few seconds, a voice recorder spoke: "This call is from a federal institution. This is a prepaid call. You will not be charged for this call. This call is from *'Johnny Ray.'* To accept this phone call, dial five now. To cancel this phone call, and any other calls from this person, press seven."

Rose quickly pressed five. "Hello," a voice said.

"Daddy, Daddy, I miss you."

"Hey, baby, your mom there?"

"No, she went to the supermarket with the boys."

"How's my queen doing?"

"I'm okay, Daddy. How you holding up in there?"

"Everything's fine. I'm maintaining."

"Daddy, I miss you so much," Rose said as she began crying.

"Stop crying, baby, everything will be all right, be strong."

"Daddy, it's just not the same without you around. I'm trying, but it's so hard."

"Put all your trust in God. Everything will turn out okay."

"Did you get the money I sent you?"

"Yes, sweetie, thank you for the hundred dollars."

"I'll send some more as soon as I can, I promise."

"Don't worry about me. Take care of your mother and brothers. I'm counting on you. Make me proud."

"I will Dad, I promise."

"What's going on with you?"

"I'm working hard, Daddy, two jobs."

"Where?"

"At the post office and at a hair salon."

"Good. I'm proud of you. Are you saving your money like I told you?"

"Yes, Daddy."

"Anything else going on?"

"I met some friends up here."

"You did? Who?"

"Some girl downstairs, named Joyce, and her family. She's cool. We work at the post office together."

"Anybody else?"

"Yeah, some guy named Eric."

"He lives there too?"

"No, he use to live here, he moved."

"What do he do?"

"Daddy, I don't know what he do, we just met."

"Okay, remember what I told you, always find out everything about any man that you think you would be interested in, and remember ..."

"I know, Daddy, never be disrespected, and never be less than a queen," Rose said, interrupting. "I won't, I promise you."

"So do you like this guy?"

"I don't know, Dad. I don't really think about it. I'm too busy working."

"Don't spin me, Rose, answer the question, you never talk

about boys."

"Daddy, I really don't know him. He's cute, he's nice, and ... and ..."

"And what?"

"And he reminds me so much of you."

"I never heard you say that about a guy before."

"No one ever made me think of you. The first time I saw Eric, I was just speechless. Everything about him reminded me of you. His complexion, his height, hair, and his beautiful smile."

"What else you ain't telling me, Rose?"

"Nothing else, Daddy, that's it."

"You sure?"

"Yes, Daddy, now listen to my poem I wrote you," Rose said, changing the subject.

"Go ahead, sweetie, I'm listening."

"It's called, *Waiting for you.*" After wiping her tears, Rose began:

"No matter how long it takes, I'll be here when you need me. Never will I turn my back, on a father that conceived me.

I dream of holding you close again, one day very soon to be there giving me away, when I finally choose a groom.

You can count on me, I'll be there to the end.

Not only are you my father, but also my best friend.

Ten years, twenty years, thirty, whatever it takes,

I'll wait for you, Dad, with all my strength, and never will I break."

Johnny Ray paused for a second ... "That was beautiful, sweetie, that was beautiful."

"Thank you, Daddy."

"I got to go now, sweetie. Tell your mother and brothers I called, and I love them, and I'll call back next week."

"Okay, Daddy, I will."

"I love you, Rose."

"I love you too, Daddy. I'll write you and send you some more money."

"Bye, bye, my love. I'm counting on you."

"Bye, Daddy," Rose said, as the phones disconnected.

Sitting back on the couch, Rose couldn't stop the flow of tears that again started falling from her beautiful brown eyes, as she thought about her father being away, doing LIFE in federal prison.

In the living room of their apartment, Eric and Braheem sat on the couch playing Sony Playstation. Larry had just left when he received a page from Bunny, the girl he met at the Platinum Club.

"Both of them was freaks," Braheem said, talking about the two women he had been with all night.

"So you had fun, huh?"

"Did I, fun ain't the word. I was like a kid in Disney World."

"All night long I was fucking them broads. I made sure I got my money's worth."

"If you put that same effort out about this money, we'll be millionaires," Eric said.

"We going to be millionaires anyway," Braheem said smiling.

"Millions don't come, you got to go get them, and then once you got 'em you got to keep 'em. Remember that," Eric said, putting his joystick down and going into his bedroom.

Sitting on his bed, Eric picked up the telephone book. As he was looking through the pages, Braheem walked in and sat beside him.

"What are you doing, Eric, with the Yellow Pages?"

"I'm looking for something."

"What?"

"Something for a friend," he said, picking up the telephone and dialing a number. "I want to do something special for a friend, something different."

"Something unexpected," Eric said, with a big smile on his face.

West Park Housing Projects...

"Keith wants to see me again," Joyce said to Rose, who was standing in the doorway.

"I thought you said that was it for him, after the other night."

"Yeah, it was, but he said I could drive his Benz, so I changed my mind," Joyce said laughing.

"Girl, you crazy."

"He's picking me up later, right outside. I told him I want all these sluts to see who's really the shit around here. Queen of the projects."

"Where are y'all going?"

"I don't know, he said something about a party with him and some friends. So you know I got to get fly tonight, I just got my Gucci outfit out of the cleaners. I'm a wear that, with my Gucci shoes and Gucci purse."

"You go, girl," Rose said.

"You should come with me, Rose. We would have so much fun."

"No, I got to work. Maybe some other time."

"Well, you know I'll tell you all the details and that won't take long. With Keith it won't be longer than five minutes," Joyce said, as they both started laughing.

"I got to pay my mom twenty dollars to babysit Ryan, so I'll probably be out all night."

The two of them then walked in the hallway. Looking down, through the open gate, they could see the tall buildings of downtown Philadelphia. As they both stood there admiring the lovely view, Rose saw the yellow cab pulling up into the project's entrance down below.

"I'll see you later, Joyce. I mean tomorrow." she said, walking down the steps.

"You be safe girl."

"I will, always, bye Rose," Joyce said as she walked back into her apartment shutting the door behind her.

That evening...

While cautiously driving down Chestnut Street, Eric looked in his rearview to make sure Braheem and Mike were close by in Braheem's car. With thirty kilos of cocaine, packed neatly inside of his Infiniti's trunk, and $100,000 in cold cash, Eric made sure they weren't too far behind. Each was holding a loaded 9 mm handgun, cocked and ready for anything suspicious. This was the worst part of the job, Eric thought. Picking up drugs from north Philly and bringing them back across the city. At any moment, anything could go wrong. Cops, stickup boys, even a simple flat tire. But it had to be done, and it had to be done by Eric. He was the one who had the drug connect with the Dominican mob from north Philly. He had been doing business with them for three years now, and he had gained their trust. Eric would buy twenty-five kilos of cocaine, sometimes even more, and they would front him whatever else he wanted. The Dominicans already had north Philly and Germantown locked down. Eric was the key to locking down west and southwest Philly, and eventually, the entire city of

Philadelphia. Pulling into the parking lot of the crib, Larry was outside waiting. Eric parked his car, and Braheem parked beside him. Getting out of his car, Eric opened his trunk and pulled out two large green trash bags. Braheem took one and Mike took the other, and all four of the men walked inside the apartment.

"Put the bags up. One of them got the money inside, take it out," Eric said.

"My bag got the money in it," Mike said, looking inside of the bag he was holding. Pulling out a small brown shopping bag, he threw it to Eric. Eric sat down on the couch in the living room and dumped the bag of money out onto the coffee table. Twenty neatly stacked hundred dollar bills laid across the table. Each stack contained five thousand dollars.

While Mike and Braheem were in the back room putting up the drugs, Larry sat next to Eric on the couch. "I told you I wanted to talk to you, Eric."

"What's up, Larry? What's so important?"

"The chick I was with last night."

"Who, the white girl?"

"Yeah, Snow Bunny. She said her brother was trying to cop something."

"Something like what?"

"She said he needed about five keez. He was looking for a new connect."

"I don't know this chick, and you don't know this chick," Eric said frowning.

"Eric, the girl is cool. Her brother hustles down south Philly, right off 7th and Snyder Avenue. She said we can meet him if we want."

"I don't think so, Larry. I never fucked with south Philly, or niggaz down S-P."

51

"It's plenty of money in south Philly," Larry said.

"What did you tell the girl?"

"I told her that I would get with my people and let her know what's up in a few days."

"What's wrong with you, Larry! Are you stupid or something! The people that we deal with now is more than enough. Business is good right now. We don't know this guy."

"I'm telling you, Eric, everything will be okay. The dude is just looking for a dependable connect, somebody who can supply his strip down south Philly. After I finished fucking the broad all night, she started telling me everything about her brother's business. She called me today and told me she told her brother about me. He's ready whenever I'm ready. I got Bunny wrapped around my finger," Larry said.

"I don't care! I said no. You should know better too, talking about our business to some stripper you just met. The answer is no, leave it alone," Eric said.

Walking back into the living room, Mike and Braheem took a seat on the couch. Turning on the large 64" T.V., Braheem then turned on the Sony Playstation video game. The four of them all grab joysticks and begin playing the addictive computer game for the remainder of the night.

Later that night at the West Park Housing Projects ...

The phone rang and Joyce picked it up immediately. "Hello."

"What's up, Joyce, it's me."

"What's up, Keith. I'm dressed. Are you on your way?"

"Yeah, I'll be there in about an hour."

"It's already 11:30 p.m. You said 11 o'clock you would be here."

"I know, sweetie, but I had to handle some B.I. I'm on my way though."

"What's up with the party?" Joyce asked.

"I changed plans. We going to chill over my man's crib with a few good friends."

"Okay, do I still get to drive?"

"No doubt, I told you, as long as you got your license pretty."

"Well, I'll see you, Keith, in an hour. Call me when you're out front."

"Peace, beautiful, I'll see you soon," Keith said hanging up.

Chapter Six

An hour later...

The project's parking lot was packed with the everyday regulars, when Keith pulled up in his platinum convertible CL 500 Mercedes Benz with the top down and the music playing a *DJ Clue* mixtape. All eyes were on this seventy-thousand dollar luxury car that most only saw in rapstar videos. But today they could see this beautiful car, right in the middle of the projects. Keith parked his car, just where Joyce had asked him to, in front of her building, so everyone could see who would be driving this expensive set of German wheels. After sliding over to the passenger side of the car, Keith took out his cell phone and called upstairs to Joyce, who had seen him when he pulled up.

"Hello," Joyce said, immediately answering the phone.

"I'm downstairs. Come on," Keith said, and hung up.

A few moments later ...

Joyce walked out of the building in her tan Gucci outfit, with matching shoes and purse. Walking past all the jealous eyes, looking ghetto fabulous, she walked in her sexiest way, displaying her thick and bow legs, as Keith just stared. Joyce walked to the Mercedes Benz, opened the door and got in. With the keys still in the ignition, she quickly put the car in reverse, backed up, put it back in drive, and drove off leaving the on-looking crowd blown away.

"We going to get something to eat first," Keith said smiling.

"Okay," Joyce said, leaning back in a relaxed position with one hand on the steering wheel and the other already gripped around Keith's dick. "Whatever you want," Joyce said, driving down Market Street.

At the Platinum Club ...

Rose had just finished her final performance for the evening. Walking in the back from off stage, her boss walked in her dressing room. Marty, a short Italian man with a long black ponytail, walked up to her. "Rose, that was great, you did a great job, beautiful."

"Thank you, Marty."

"You're our number one dancer. All the men wait around to see you perform."

"Thanks, I do my best," Rose said rubbing her aching feet.

"Did you think about what I asked you?"

"Yeah, and the answer is still no Marty. I don't want to have sex with your boss. I don't care what he will pay me."

"But Mr. Perotta said he would give you an extra fifteen hundred on that five thousand, that's sixty-five hundred dollars, Rose."

"Even though I could really use the money, Marty, tell Mr. Perotta that my answer is still no. If he had a daughter, he would understand."

"Okay, I'll tell him," Marty said walking out of the dressing room, shaking his head.

Picking up the telephone, Rose called for a cab to come pick her up and take her and her aching feet home. After taking off her outfit, she put on her red Air Nikes, a pair of Calvin Klein jeans, a red Gap sweatshirt, and walked out the side door to wait for her cab. Walking outside, a white Cadillac Limousine was parked with a chauffeur waiting with the limo door already open.

"Here go, Rose," a female said, walking with two other girls.

"Excuse me. Are you Rose?" the man asked.

"Yes, why? Who wants to know?"

"I was sent to escort you home tonight."

"What! By who?" she said, smiling, thinking he was mistaken.

Pulling out a small piece of paper, "Eric. Eric paid for it."

"Oh, my God, that boy is crazy," Rose said, shaking her head.

"Where is he?"

"I don't know, ma'am, I was just told to be here by two o'clock and ask for Rose. That she would be the most beautiful woman who walked out this door," he said, pointing to the side door.

"Oh, my God. I don't believe him. That boy will not give up," Rose said smiling.

Pulling up behind the limo, a cab driver yelled from out his window. "Are you Rose?"

"Yes," she said, walking over to him.

"I'm so sorry, but I have a ride. Someone's taking me home," she said.

"I drove all the way from 21st and Christian for this," he said in an upset voice.

Going into her pocket, Rose pulled out a twenty dollar bill.

"Here sir, calm down," she said, passing the cab driver the money.

"Thank you, pretty," he said, immediately pulling off, after hearing over the radio about another customer in need of his service.

Rose walked back to the waiting chauffeur and got inside the limo.

"Who're you?" she said, setting back on the soft Cadillac seat.

"My name is Maria," the middle-aged Spanish woman said, rubbing her hands together with some type of lotion. "I'm a masseuse, a certified massage therapist."

"What! No, he didn't. I don't believe that boy. Are you serious?"

"Yes, now can you take off your sneakers?"

Rose sat back speechless, as she shook her head in total amazement. Never had any man ever done anything like this for her. This was stuff she thought only happened in fairytales. But right now, it was happening in real life. And she was enjoying every moment. Slowly, the limo pulled off.

"Oh, here," Maria said, after putting both of Rose's feet across her lap. "This is yours," she said, passing her a white card with a picture of a yellow rose on the cover.

Opening up the card, pieces of rose petals fell out onto her lap. "Oh, my God, I do not believe this boy," she said reading the original poem that had been written especially for her.

I Can Feel It ...

"The first time I ever saw you, my mind was blown away.

My heart had a million questions, but my tongue was so captivated by your beauty, it remained speechless.

I thought I was dreaming, until I touched myself. Then I knew you were real.

For a moment my heart stopped, but once you spoke, it began to beat again. I can't keep my mind off you, and if I could, I wouldn't. I would let your picture stay in my head forever. Waking up in the morning with you, and at night taking you to bed.

I can feel it in my soul, that we're made for each other.
I can feel my spirit being called in your direction.
I can feel it ..."

Rose sat back and looked at the lady massaging her feet, shaking her head. All she could do was smile and shed a tear. From all the poetry she had written for people, this was the first time anyone had written a poem for her.

Twenty minutes later ...

The limo pulled up in front of the Marriott Hotel in center city and parked. Rose had just put back on her sneakers, wondering why the limo had suddenly stopped. The chauffeur then walked around to the side door of the limo and opened it up.

"This is yours," he said, handing Rose a key with a small tag on it that said, "Room **421** Executive Suite."

"What's this?" Rose said, getting out of the limo, watching the hotel's doorman hold open the door.

"This is where I was told to bring you, ma'am," the chauffeur said.

"No, he didn't. I know he don't think because I dance and he spent a few dollars on a limo that he expects me to sleep with him."

Rose's smile quickly turned to a frown and her tears quickly stopped. Mad and upset, Rose walked through the hotel lobby to the elevator. Getting off on the 4th floor, she walked down the hallway until she came across "Suite **421**." Using the key, she opened the door and walked in. A trail of rose petals covered the floor. She screamed his name. "Eric," but there was no answer. Angrily, she walked into the master bedroom and turned on the light. The sight of an all-white teddy bear brought a smile back to her pretty face. As she glanced to her left, she noticed a bubbling Jacuzzi and an ice bucket full of Dom Perignon sitting on a cart with a bowl of fresh fruit. Walking to the bed, Rose saw a note laying next to the teddy bear. Picking it up, she began to read it. ***"Dear Rose,*** *I hope you don't think I over did it, but I'm the type who could never start something without finishing it proper. The suite is paid for, along with room service for the entire night. The limo will be out front in the morning to take you back home. Please enjoy yourself, and if you get lonely, Teddy will keep you company.*

−Eric"

Rose grabbed her white teddy bear and just laid across the bed. Kicking off her sneakers, she also took off her sweatshirt and just threw it on the floor. After calling her mother, telling her she would be home in the morning, Rose took off the remainder of her clothes and got into the bubbling Jacuzzi that her tired body was craving for. Never had Rose experienced anything like this in her short twenty years of living, she had thought to herself. And at the same time, never had she felt so afraid in all her life.

At the same time ...

On the opposite side of town, Keith and Joyce had just come from drinking, eating and shopping down South Street. It was the only street in Philly that would still be open til four or five in the morning for its late night center city customers. Half drunk and sleepy, Joyce put her bags in the trunk of the car and followed Keith into a house. Walking inside, she observed two men sitting on the sofa watching T.V. The two guys got up and followed Keith into the kitchen, while Joyce took a seat on the sofa, barely able to stay awake. After a few moments, Keith walked back out alone. After whispering in Joyce's ear, the two of them walked up the steps and into a room.

"Who was those guys?" Joyce asked, staggering.

"Oh, they just friends." Keith said, kissing Joyce down her neck, while undressing her.

After Joyce was totally naked, she laid across the bed, and Keith, who was also fully undressed, began performing oral sex on her. After fifteen minutes of kissing and sucking Joyce's hairy pussy, Keith turned Joyce around and began fucking her from behind.

"Oh, girl, you got the best pussy in the world," he said as he was deeply stroking, while at the same time pulling on her long black hair, never noticing the video recorder that was sitting on top of the T.V. recording everything.

Joyce's intense moans began to fill the room. **"Ohh, ohh, Keith,"** she said, **"Ohh, ya dick feels so good,"** at the same time, the two guys from downstairs both walked into the bedroom, both, butt ass naked, with the look of starving lions on their faces. Half drunk and confused to what was happening, Keith and one of the guys quickly grabbed Joyce and held her naked body down. After one of the guys punched her in the face, leaving her now half dazed, her struggles and screams became meaningless. One at a time, they all took turns raping Joyce repeatedly.

"This is what you want, bitch. This is how you like it," Keith said, holding Joyce down, as one of the guys began inserting himself inside her anus. Scared and in pain, Joyce closed her eyes. With tears rolling down her face, Joyce knew she could do nothing but wish it would soon hurry up and end.

Chapter Seven

Sunday morning service ... the next day.

At St. Mary's Baptist Church, Rose and her family all sat together in the middle row of the crowded place of worship. The choir had just finished singing a moving version of *"Amazing Grace."* The preacher then opened his bible and started reading.

"Excuse me," a young man said, walking through the crowded aisles.

Looking up, Rose noticed Eric walking down her row towards her. "Oh, no!" she said smiling. "Oh, I don't believe him."

"Slide over." Eric said, taking a seat between her and her mother. "Hi you doing, ma'am, my name is Eric. I'm a friend of Rose's." he said shaking her hand, showing all his white teeth.

"Oh, you must be the one who kept her out all night," Rose's mother said, smiling at the both of them.

"Yeah, you can say that," Eric said, smiling.

Rose just shook her head, blushing from head to toe.

"Now I see where you get your beautiful looks from," Eric

said.

"Oh, thank you," Rose's mother said, blushing at the compliment.

Dressed in a blue Italian made suit, Eric pulled out his small black bible. "Do you know where the preacher's at?" he asked Rose's very impressed mother.

"The Book of Job," she said smiling.

"Oh, my favorite book in the bible. The man who lost everything, but with his faith in God, he was given it all back, plus double."

Rose sat speechless in her seat while Eric paid her no mind, looking straight ahead at the minister who was preaching. All she could do was sit in her seat and smile, unable to figure this man out.

Dropping Joyce off in front of the projects, Keith quickly pulled off. Holding her bags of clothes in both hands, Joyce painfully walked through the project's door and up the twelve long flights of stairs. Entering her apartment, she saw her son Ryan asleep on the sofa. After putting her bags down, she walked into the bathroom and shut the door. Looking into the mirror for the first time, she saw her bruised eye. After locking the bathroom door, Joyce took off all her clothes and turned on the shower. Getting under the warm water, she washed away all the filth that had covered her sore and bruised body. As her tears rolled down her face, a small trail of blood from her anus rolled down her legs, onto the floor of the tub. After washing and drying herself off, Joyce put on clean underwear and a tee-shirt and layed her aching body on the sofa next to Ryan and cried herself to sleep.

An hour later...

Everyone stood around outside talking after the church service was over. Eric pulled his car in front of the church and rolled down the window. "Come on, I'll drop y'all off," he said to Rose and her family, who were about to catch a bus back home. Her two little bothers quickly ran and jumped into the back of the car. Rose's mother got in the back and then shut the door, while Rose sat up front with Eric.

"Thank you, Eric, but you didn't have to," she said.

"Oh, yes I did," he said, driving down the street.

"Are y'all hungry?" he asked her mother and brothers, who were all enjoying the smooth ride of the Infinity Q45.

"Yeah, yeah, we hungry," both boys yelled at the same time.

"No, they're just greedy," Rose said in an angry voice.

"I could use something to eat," Rose's mother said.

"Chuckie Cheeze, McDonald's, Burger King," the boys both shouted.

"How about some blueberry pancakes," Eric said, smiling.

"Oh weee, yeeeh, pancakes," the boys quickly changed their minds.

"Okay, we're all going to IHOP," Eric said getting on the expressway. "International House of Pancakes, here we come," Eric said.

With a frown on her face, Rose crossed her arms like a spoiled brat.

"Smile, girl, cheer up. You can have some pancakes too," Eric said, as everyone started laughing, including Rose.

Hearing his cell phone ring, Eric picked it up and answered it. "Hello."

"What's up, E. It's me, Mike. I been calling you all morning."

"I didn't have my phone on me. What's up?"

"Are you going by the Belmont Plateau with me, Larry and Braheem?"

"No, not today. I'm busy. Y'all go have fun. Maybe next week."

"All right, E, I'll see you later," Mike said as they both hung up at the same time.

A few moments later ...

Eric pulled into the International House of Pancakes' parking lot. After finding a parking space, they all got out of the car and went into the restaurant.

"Mom, you and the boys can go order. I got to talk to Eric for a minute," Rose said.

Her mother and brothers walked into the back of the restaurant to find a seat. Eric stood there wondering what could it be that Rose wanted to talk about.

"Eric, why? Tell me why, Eric?" Rose said, looking him straight in his dark brown eyes.

"Why, what?"

"Why me? Why all of this? Why are you doing this?"

"I told you why, in the poem I wrote you."

"Eric, you're scaring me. I don't know what you want from me."

"Rose, I have everything in life that I could ever want, except one thing."

"And what's that, Eric?"

"Your heart."

"Eric, please, you're confusing me."

Eric reached out and grabbed Rose's hand. "Rose, what would you do if I kissed you right now?"

"I would smack you."

Eric laughed and said, "That's a chance I would have to take."

Suddenly, Eric gently pulled Rose into his arms and passionately began kissing her on her soft red lips. Even if she wanted to smack him, the feeling of Eric's soft lips against hers felt too good to pull away. So she just remained captivated in his arms until he finished.

"Why did you do that?"

"Because I been waiting to kiss you ever since I first laid eyes on you," and without blinking, Eric looked straight into her eyes.

Rose said nothing, as she just walked back and sat at the table with her family.

As Eric took a seat next to Rose, she leaned over and whispered in his ear. "Okay, well there's some very important things you need to know."

"What?" Eric said.

"We'll talk, but not right now," she said, grabbing a menu off the table.

"When?"

"Soon, Mr. Persistence, very soon," she said smiling.

After breakfast, Eric dropped Rose and her family off back home. Rose had promised to call him later and the two of them would go out to dinner and finish their conversation. There was something Eric needed to know, and Rose felt there was no need to beat around the bush any longer.

Later that afternoon ...

Sitting in the living room watching T.V., the phone rang and Rose picked it up. "Hello," she answered.

"Hey, Rose."

"Hey, Joyce, what's up girl?"

"Can you come over? I need to talk to you," Joyce said in a sad voice.

"What's wrong?"

"Just can you please come over. I'll tell you when you get here."

"I'm on my way down," Rose said, hanging up the phone.

Putting on her sneakers, Rose quickly ran out the door and downstairs to Joyce's apartment. Knocking on the door, Joyce yelled for her to come in. Rose walked in. Walking out from a bedroom with dark shades on, Joyce took a seat on the living room sofa. Rose sat down next to her.

"What's up girl? Why you sound like that on the phone?"

Lifting up her shades, Joyce began to cry on Rose's shoulder. "I was raped! They raped me last night, Rose."

"Who raped you! Tell me who! Joyce, are you okay?"

"I'm fine. I'm just glad it's over."

"Who did it?"

"It was Keith! Keith and two of his friends. They all raped me."

"I'm going to call the cops," Rose said reaching for the telephone.

"No! No! I'm okay. No cops, please. I don't want my family to know anything about this."

"Well, you can't just let it go, just like that."

"I'm okay, just a little sore."

"Well, at least let me tell Eric."

"No! Please not Eric. He would kill Keith and his friends. I don't want Eric getting into no trouble over me. Please, don't tell Eric."

"But you just can't do nothing."

"I'm okay, Rose, I just needed to talk to somebody, and I

knew that you would listen. Please just let it go."

"No, no, get dressed, Joyce, right now," Rose said, standing up.

"Why?"

"We are going to the hospital. You need to be checked out."

"I'm okay, Rose."

"Either get dressed or I'm calling Eric right now."

"But ..."

"No buts, just put on your clothes."

As Joyce walked into her bedroom to get dressed, Rose called a cab. After Joyce was dressed, they both walked downstairs and waited for the cab to come and take them to the hospital.

Twenty minutes later ...

The cab pulled up and both women got in. Sitting in the back of the cab, neither woman said a word. Total silence was inside the cab the entire ride to the hospital.

Fairmount Park ...

The Belmont Plateau was packed. All the hustlers and ballers were out that day, showing off their freshly washed cars and motorcycles. The temperature was around 85° on that warm Sunday afternoon. Women in tight shorts seemed to be all over the place while all the hungry male predators followed closely behind. This was the spot in Philly where every and anybody, male or female, would be on Sunday afternoons. A ghetto car and fashion show is what it was. Mike, Larry and Braheem all drove slowly behind each other. The sight of the cherry red Lexus coupe, smoke silver Mercedes Benz, and money green convertible BMW had all the women staring hard, while all the men looked out the side of their eye at the three luxury cars flowing through the banging stereo systems, each sitting on 20" rims. As all three cars pulled to the side of the road, about twenty females all rushed around them. And the women who didn't come, wished they were one of the twenty that knew these young ghetto fabulous hustlers.

"Where's Eric?" a beautiful half-Philippino and black woman said.

"He's chilling today, Seini," Braheem said, with his arms around another beautiful female's waist.

"Why didn't you call me, Larry?" another gorgeous dark-skinned sister in tight shorts and a soaking wet tee-shirt, showing her erected nipples, said smiling.

"I did call you. Ya sister ain't tell you?"

"I don't have a sister. I got a brother," she said, as everyone burst out laughing.

This is how every Sunday at the Belmont Plateau would be when they would all show up dressed in the flyest clothes, sporting their expensive iced out Rolex and Cartier watches. This was the life, young, paid, and got it made. But Eric had schooled each of his soldiers about this cruel game of **Money, Desire, and Regrets**. Numerous times he had told them about the benefits of the game, money, sex, power, respect, but never without telling them about the negative sides as well. Violence, pain, and sometimes even death. So each one of them was well aware of this ghetto fabulous lifestyle that they were all living. Knowing that every woman was out there looking for a potential baby daddy, while every nigga was looking for a potential homicide victim. It's sad, but it's real.

Later that night...

Rose and Joyce walked back into Joyce's apartment after just leaving the hospital. "You'll be okay. You're lucky. Those guys could have had anything. Take the pills the doctor gave you and soak like he said."

"Do you think the doctor knew I was raped?"

"Probably, but if you don't say you was raped, he can't report it."

"What about my eye?" Joyce said.

"You told him that you got into a fight with your sister. He don't know. He said you have a mild detachment of the retina and it should heal on its own, in a few weeks and to come back if things got worse."

"Thank you, Rose, thank you very much. I'm so glad to have a friend like you."

"It's nothing, you would have done the same for me, but you need to slow down, Joyce. This was a learning lesson. You are a beautiful girl and very bright. You should really start evaluating your life. Don't let these niggaz break you girl. You have a son and two younger sisters who look up to you. Start being a role model, not only for them, but also for yourself," Rose said.

Joyce said nothing as she stood there with tears running down her face. Coming from out of the back room, her son Ryan ran to his mother's arms. "Mommy, Mommy," Ryan said, as Joyce picked him up.

Walking to the door, Rose paused. "That's all that should matter to you, raising that cute little boy," she said as she walked out the door shutting it behind her.

Walking upstairs to her own apartment, Rose immediately grabbed the phone and called Eric.

"Hello," Eric said, answering his cell phone.

"Hi, Eric, it's me, Rose."

"What took you so long? I thought we were going out to dinner."

"I'm sorry, something came up."

"Is everything okay?"

"Yes, I'm fine. I just had to help a friend of mine, but she's okay now."

"What's up? Do you still want to go to dinner?"

"No, but I would like to talk to you."

"When?"

"Right now."

"I'll be there in fifteen minutes."

"I'll be standing outside when you pull up."

"I'm on my way. Bye, Rose."

"Bye, Eric," Rose said, hanging up the phone.

Walking into the back room, Rose opened up her mother's bedroom door. Seeing her mother asleep and under the covers, she quietly closed it back. Walking over to her little brothers' room, she opened the door and they too were asleep. Rose walked out and sat down at the kitchen table. Suddenly, a smile appeared on her face. "Everything will be okay y'all," she said to herself. "Everyone will be okay, I promise," she said as she got up and walked out the door.

Fifteen minutes later...

Rose was standing in the project's doorway when Eric pulled up. Walking towards his car, he opened the door and she got in.

"Can we go for a ride?"

"Yeah, where?"

"Anywhere."

"Okay, beautiful. I know the place," Eric said, backing out of the lot and driving away.

Looking at Rose, Eric could see the serious look on her face, but he said nothing, not one word. He knew she would be doing all the talking tonight.

A few moments later...

Eric parked his car by an empty bench in Fairmount Park, not too far from Kelly's swimming pool. The dark sky was full of bright beautiful stars on this calm spring night. The temperature had dropped to the mid 60s. A few other people had been sitting around on other benches, around this small pond that was only a few feet away. Getting out of the car, Eric and Rose both took a seat on the bench.

"What did you want to talk about?" Eric said.

"Eric, there's something you need to know."

"Go ahead, I'm ready."

"Eric, you were right when you said that the first time we saw each other, you thought that something was special. You felt something. I'll be serious, Eric, when I first saw you in your car that day, I couldn't believe how fine you were, but I said nothing. I just let you talk. My father had always told me never say a word when a man opens his mouth. He'll answer all your questions for you. Everything about you I like, everything except you being a drug dealer. But when Joyce told me how you would drop off money to help her and her family, I knew you were different. I knew you were not like the typical drug dealer-hustler running around flaunting his materialistic items, showing off. I knew you were a different kind of man. When you did the things you did, the limo, the hotel, the massage therapist,

I was on cloud nine, dreamland, *Dorothy* in the *Wizard of Oz*. When I read your poem, I could do nothing but cry, the last three lines when you said, *'I can feel it in my soul, that we're made for each other. I can feel my spirit being called in your direction, I can feel it ...'* was exactly how I felt. In all my twenty years, never had words touched me the way yours had. Still I was unsure of your intentions. That was until you walked inside my church. I did not have to question you anymore. I was hooked. The limo and hotel were cute, and don't get me wrong, I loved every minute of it, but when you sat between me and my mother at church and pulled out your bible, that was the icing on the cake. I want you to know, Eric, that yes, I really was confused, but now I'm not. I want you. Just as bad as you probably want me. But there are things you need to know and respect, if you want to be with me, and want me to be all yours."

"What's that, Rose, tell me," Eric said.

"First, Eric, if you can't love me and only me, get up and walk away now."

Eric smiled.

"If you ever put your hands on me, I'm out, it's that simple. I want you to know that you do not have to lie to me; we can talk about anything. Don't ever try to change me, and do not try and buy my love. My love is priceless."

"That's it?" Eric said.

"No, two more things."

"What's that?"

"You have to meet my father. My father is my heart, my world."

"What else, Rose?" Eric said, looking straight into her eyes.

Rose paused for a second, then stood up and looked Eric in his eyes. "You might not believe this, but I'm still a virgin."

73

"What!" Eric said. "What did you say?"

"You heard me. I'm still a virgin, is that a problem?"

"No. I think it's beautiful, the best news of the day," Eric said. "But what about you stripping?"

"I will quit, when I'm ready. I know you don't want me dancing, and I know you're probably surprised at the way I dance, and still being a virgin."

Eric stood there shaking his head.

"Well, I just always enjoyed dancing. When I'm up on that stage, I'm not dancing for the men who break their necks to see me, half naked, I'm dancing for me, myself."

Eric stood up, took off his jacket, and put it around Rose's shoulders. "All I know is that I want you, more than I ever wanted any woman. I don't care if you are poor, a stripper, or even a virgin. All I know is that my heart don't lie, and I want you, Rose."

"You got me, Eric, you got me," she said, as they passionately began kissing under the bright beautiful stars that sat high above the sky shining down on the two of them.

Chapter Eight

Monday evening ...

The silver Mercedes Benz drove onto the 6th Street parkway garage. Finding a place to park, Larry got out of his car and walked up to the two guys who had been waiting.

"Hi you doing. I'm Mario," the short, stocky built Italian man said. "This is my friend, Vinny."

Larry shook both guys' hands and the three all walked inside the garage.

"So will it be a problem? Can you handle it, L?"

"Five birds, no problem. That's small. When will y'all be ready?"

"As soon as possible, tomorrow if possible."

"Tomorrow is fine. I'll call you and set up a time and place to meet."

"Right here," Vinny said.

"Here?" Larry said, looking around.

"Yeah, this is my uncle's garage. I run it. It's safe."

"Okay, this place is fine. You remember the price, right?"

"Twenty thousand a chicken, $100,000 for five," Mario said.

"Deal," Larry said as they all walked back outside.

Getting back into his car, Larry cut the engine on and rolled down the window. "I'll call you tomorrow, Mario."

"I look forward to doing business with you, L," he said as Larry drove out of the parking lot and up the street. Driving down the street, Larry called Eric on his cell phone.

"Hello."

"What's up, E?"

"Where you at? You know you supposed to be here at the crib, it's Monday."

"I'm on my way now. I had to drop some money off over my baby's mom's."

"I'll see you when you get here, Larry," Eric said, angrily hanging up.

Larry hung up the phone and smiled, as he drove down the street. He had just come up on a few extra thousand dollars. Eric would charge him $17,000 a kilo. Kilos that Eric had been getting for $14,000 a piece from the Dominicans. Now Larry would be making himself a $3,000 dollar profit off of Mario, like Eric had been making off of him. That would be $15,000 extra dollars that Larry would be keeping all to himself, every time Mario would buy five. And even making more money if Mario needed more.

At the crib ...

Eric, Braheem and Mike all sat around the kitchen table. "Here, Mike, this is yours," he said, passing him a large trash bag containing ten kilos of Columbia's finest export.

"I'm out," Mike said, putting the bag on his shoulder.

"Braheem, walk him to his car and make sure everything is okay."

"All right, Eric," Braheem said, following Mike out the door. At the same time, Larry was walking in.

"What's up, E?"

"Nigga, what's wrong with you? You know on Mondays

we handle our business and everything else supposed to be taken care of already."

"I'm sorry, E, but I had an emergency with my baby's mom, you know how they can get."

"No, I don't. I don't have a baby's mom."

"I'm sorry, E, I'll make sure it won't happen again. What's up?"

"Here, Larry, this is yours," Eric said, passing him another bag that was laying by his side.

"What's this?"

"Fifteen keez, your strip has been doing good. You needed to step up so I gave you five extra."

"Thanks, E," Larry said, grabbing the bag and walking to the door.

"Larry, hold up one minute."

"Yeah, E, what's up?"

"You remember our talk right?"

"Eric, you said what you said, and I respect that. I would never cross you."

"Remember that," Eric said. "Never cross the family and we'll eat forever."

"I will talk to you later, E," Larry said as he rushed out the door.

A few moments later, Braheem walked back inside.

"What's up with Larry?"

"Why? What's wrong?"

"Nothing, he just drove off like a bat out of hell. He must got a date or something, only one thing makes him break his neck like that, PUSSY!," Braheem said, as he sat down and started laughing. "What's wrong, Eric?"

"I'm worried about Larry."

"Why? What's wrong?"

"The other day he told me about some chick who's brother wanted to buy something."

"What's wrong with that, that's what we do."

"Yeah, but he don't know this dude. It's that stripper he met at the Platinum Club, brother."

"The white girl?"

"Yeah."

"Well, what did you tell him?"

"I told him to leave it alone, that we don't know them, so that was that."

"Well, you know pussy can turn a saint to a sinner, but you shouldn't worry about Larry, he knows better."

"I hope so, Braheem, I hope you're right."

"Now what's up with this shorty you want us to meet tomorrow?" Braheem said.

A smile quickly appeared on Eric's face. "Everyone will all meet her tomorrow."

"Is it somebody we know?"

"Nope, so don't ask no more questions, you will all see tomorrow, after I take her by my mother's house."

"She better be all that, especially if you taking her to meet aunty."

"You'll see," Eric said, putting his arms around Braheem. "You'll see."

The two of them went into the living room. Turning on his cell phone, Eric called Rose.

"Hello," she answered.

"Hey, boo."

"Hey, Eric. I was just talking about you to my mother and I told my father earlier that we would come visit him next Saturday."

"Okay, so what was you and your mom talking about?"

"She just said she likes you and that you was cute."

"Tell Mom I said thanks." Eric said smiling.

"I will. What's up baby?"

"I'm on my way over to take you to work. I'll be there in about a half hour."

"Okay, I'll see you when you get here, Eric, bye." Rose said.

"Bye, boo," at the same time, they both hung up.

Braheem sat there shaking his head. "You soft nigga. Bye boo, baby, man she better be all that," he said, turning on the T.V. and video game. "She better be all that."

Eric grabbed a joystick and smiled. "You'll see. You'll see tomorrow," Eric confidently said with a big smile on his face.

Chapter Eight

Tuesday afternoon...

Eric and Rose had just left his mother's home in southwest Philly and were on their way to meet the guys at his apartment. Driving into the parking lot of his apartment complex, he parked and he and Rose got out of the car. "This is beautiful. It's nice out here," Rose said, looking around at the nice scenery that she had missed since moving to the projects. "It reminds me of Cherry Hill."

"Thank you," Eric said as they both walked through the door of his apartment.

Sitting on the living room sofa, Mike, Larry and Braheem's eyes almost all seemed to pop through their heads.

"Hey, you Extacy." Larry said, smiling, rubbing his eyes to make sure it was her.

"Her name is Rose. Rose, this is Larry, this is Mike, and this is my little cousin Braheem," he said, introducing them all.

"Aw man, E. You right man, she is beautiful," Braheem said.

"Thank you," Rose said blushing.

"You got any sisters?" Mike said. "Any cousins or anything?"

"No, just brothers," she said, smiling.

"Aw man, God only made one of you," Larry said.

"Yup, just one," Eric said, putting his arms around Rose.

"Well, Rose, this is my other family. You met my mother and little brother, these three knuckleheads are the rest of my family."

Giving Rose his keys, Eric asked her to go to the car and wait for him. After walking out and shutting the door behind her, the questions began.

"E, how did you pull that?" Mike asked.

"Damn dogg."

"A long story," Eric said smiling.

"You lucky ass nigga, damn she is fine as hell," Larry said, looking out the window watching her get into the car.

"That's who you waited for at the club that night," Braheem said.

"Yup, that's why I waited."

"Why do she have on that post office jacket?" Mike asked.

"That's where she works. I picked her up on her lunch break."

"I can't front, E. She is a dime, all day long."

"She's like Halle Berry and Jennifer Lopez, mixed together," Larry said. "No wonder you ain't come out to the Belmont Plateau with us," Braheem said.

"And I won't be going out to the Plateau no more, unless I'm with my shorty. I'm cutting all them chicken heads off," Eric said.

"I don't blame you. You done got like Joe," Mike said.

"What's that?" Eric said.

"You don't want to be a player no more," Braheem said as they all bust out laughing.

"I'll see y'all later," Eric said, walking out the door leaving all three of them standing there speechless, shaking their heads.

Getting into his car, Eric sat down. "What do they think?"

Rose said smiling.

"They said you was okay. I could have done better."

"What!" Rose said frowning.

"Girl, you know them niggaz tripping over you," Eric said, laughing as Rose suddenly began smiling. "Now let me take you back to work, before you get fired," he said, pulling off and driving away.

Later that evening, at Mario's uncle's garage in south Philly, Larry with his 9 mm tucked on his waist, cautiously dumped five tightly wrapped kilos of cocaine from out of a grey backpack onto a table. Mario grabbed a small knife from off a tool shelf and cut open one of the kilos of cocaine. With his right index finger, he put a small amount on its tip then tasted it with his tongue. The pureness of the cocaine numbed his tongue instantly. He then looked at Vinny, who was standing next to him, and shook his head, confirming that the product was good.

"I told you, it's the best shit in the city," Larry said smiling.

Vinny then dumped out a bag of neatly wrapped money, ten stacks all together. "It's $100,000 dollars, count it," Vinny said.

"I don't need to count it, I believe it's all there," Larry said putting the money inside his backpack.

"We'll be calling you in a few days," Mario said.

"I'll be waiting, all you got to do is page me, whatever you need, I got."

"We look forward to doing a lot of business with you, L," Vinny said, shaking Larry's hand.

"And I look forward to establishing a great relationship with y'all gentlemen," Larry said, with all the money now inside the backpack. Vinny and Mario walked Larry to the door and watched him as he walked to his car, got in, and drove off.

Walking back inside the garage, Vinny and Mario stood around the pounds of cocaine that were spread on the table. "This is some good shit, Vinny," Mario said, holding a kilo in his hand.

"Yeah, we need to buy as much of this as we can. Coke this good don't be around long."

A few days later, Larry met Vinny and Mario again at the garage, this time selling them ten kilos of cocaine. Twenty-five kilos was what Vinny and Mario wanted to get off Larry the next time they met. A quantity that Larry had agreed to have ready for them. The only problem was that Eric only gave enough for his drug strip, and that was usually 10 to 15 kilos at a time. Larry knew he would have to figure out a way to get more kilos from Eric, without Eric getting suspicious and finding out about Mario. He knew he would have to think of something soon. Vinny and Mario were expecting him to have the 25 kilos in a week. Larry knew if he could produce the 5 kilos, that they would want even more the next time around. And soon he wouldn't have to be under Eric, but on the same level as Eric. Something that had always been in the back of his mind.

Lewisburg Maximum Penitentiary, upstate Pennsylvania...

The visiting room was packed with women and children on this Saturday afternoon. Rose and Eric waited on a bench for Johnny Ray to come out. Moments later, Rose spotted her father walking out from the inmates' entrance into the crowded room. "Daddy, Daddy," she said, yelling his name and running up to him.

It had been over six months since the two of them had seen each other, their longest separation since Johnny Ray had been incarcerated. Usually, Rose and the family would come up once a month, but times had gotten rough over the last few months causing them to limit their monthly visits. Tears began to fall down Rose's face. Whenever she would see her father dressed in prison clothes, she was instantly reminded of him never coming home again, and spending the rest of his life behind those cold steel bars.

"How's my baby girl doing?"

"I'm fine, Daddy. I miss you so much." she said as they both walked to the bench where Eric was sitting.

"Daddy, this is Eric, who I told you about."

Eric stood up and shook Johnny Ray's hand.

"Hi you doing, son? I been looking forward to meeting you."

"I'm fine," Eric said, staring at an older image of himself.

"So you're Eric. I heard good things about you."

Eric said nothing, neither did Rose as they all sat down on the bench.

"My wife said you are a nice kid and my sons seem to think highly of you as well. So tell me, Eric, do you have any children?"

"Daddy," Rose said, interrupting.

"It's okay, Rose," Eric said. "No sir, no. I don't have any kids."

"Oh, then you could never understand a love of a parent, huh?"

"I guess not, not until I have some children."

"Well, Eric, I have three. but only one girl."

"I understand."

"No, I don't think you understand, son." Standing up,

Johnny Ray asked Rose to go to the soda machines and get them all a soda. She knew the real reason was to talk to Eric alone, and Eric knew too. Rose got up and walked through the crowd. Johnny Ray sat back down and looked Eric in the eyes.

"Eric, I want you to know one thing, my friend. That girl is my heart, and if you ever break her heart, then you break my heart."

"Sir, you don't have to worry about ..."

"Listen here, Eric," Johnny Ray said, interrupting, "as long as I'm in here doing life, away from my family, I'm going to be worrying. I don't know what you do, but looking at you it don't take long to figure it out, so don't bullshit me son. My daughter must really like you if she brought you to meet me, and I really hope you feel the same as her."

"I do, I care about Rose a lot."

"You know what, Eric? I believe you. I seen the way y'all both looked on the bench when I came out. I can tell there's something special between the two of you."

"Eric, whatever you are doing on them streets, I want you to look at me, look me right in my eyes. This could easily be you."

"I know. I think about it all the time," Eric said.

"Son, this game we play is real. If you're not one of the few lucky ones who get out, only two things come from this, and that's **LIFE or DEATH**, either one, you lose."

"The game is not the same, ever since the players changed."

"I had two homes, one in Jersey and one in Virginia, cars, jewelry, clothes, and fame. You name it, and I had it, and just like that, I lost everything. The feds froze my accounts, seized my cars, and all my property. They took everything that wasn't nailed down. I been locked up for five years, missing my two sons and daughter growing up, knowing that I will never walk out of these gates again. If you care for my daughter like you said, I ask you to do me one favor, Eric."

"What's that, sir?"

"To never take her through what I did to her mother. You still have a chance, all my chances are long gone. All I ask you to do is the right thing, and please don't end up another statistic, behind bars, or in the dirt."

Eric sat there, thinking about everything that Johnny Ray had just said.

Walking back up with three Pepsi colas, Rose sat back down. "Here, Daddy," she said, passing him one of the ice cold sodas. "And here's yours, Eric. They're cold too," she said, feeling the tension on the bench.

"What was y'all two talking about?"

"Men stuff," Johnny Ray said, opening up his soda.

"What's men stuff, Daddy?"

"Stuff only between men," he said looking at Eric.

"Okay, y'all don't have to tell me."

"So, what has my little girl been doing?" Johnny Ray said, changing the subject.

"Working hard, Daddy, two jobs has been killing me."

"Things will get better, sweetie."

"I know, at least I don't have to catch the bus no more. Eric takes me and picks me up from work."

"Thank you, Eric."

"It's nothing, sir."

"Call me Johnny Ray. Sir sound old, I'm only 38. By the way, you'll be 21 soon."

"It's still three months away," Rose said, smiling, happy that he had remembered.

"Eric, how old are you?"

"I'm 22. I'll be 23 on the fourth of July."

Rose and Johnny Ray both looked at each other and started laughing.

"What?" Eric said, "what's so funny?"

"That's Rose's birthday. She's an Independence Day baby too."

"What! For real?" Eric said, shaking his head in disbelief.

"I don't believe it," Rose said smiling.

"Maybe you two was meant to be," Johnny Ray said. "But only time will tell. Only time will tell."

For the remaining visiting time, the three of them all sat around talking. When visiting was over, Rose had promised to be back up in a month. And Eric had promised to come back with her.

"Your father loves you to death," Eric said, driving on the expressway back home.

"I know. He reminds me all the time."

"He's a cool oldhead."

"He's okay. He's just Daddy."

"So what are we going to do for our birthday?" Eric said, changing the subject.

"I'm sure you'll think of something, now that you know our birthdays are on the same day."

"Yeah, that's still trippin me out. Who would ever believe that both our birthdays are on the fourth of July?"

"I know, it's crazy, ain't it?" Rose said smiling.

"But maybe it's fate," she said staring at Eric as he drove. "Maybe it's fate."

Chapter Ten

Sunday afternoon...

Larry and Mike were sitting on the sofa in the living room of the crib. "What is so important, Larry?"

"I needed to talk to you, Mike."

"About what?"

"Business. Money."

"You been making all the money. So what's wrong?"

"Nothing, that's why I needed to talk to you, Mike."

"Well, stop beating around the bush, nigga, and tell me what's up."

"I got this hookup with these Italians."

"Are those the guys Eric told you not to mess with?"

"Yeah, but Mike, I been making a killing. I made $45,000 this week."

"How much?"

"Forty-five G's."

"You know, if Eric finds out, he will go off, Larry."

"I know, but he won't ever find out."

"You better hope he never does, Larry."

"I'm telling you, Mike, it's sweet. Them suckers are buying bricks for 20 thousand a piece, everyone I sell them, I'm making three G's. Now they need 25 kilos next week. Eric will only give me 15. I need your 10. We can split the profit."

"I don't know, L. Eric said never to cross him man. And never let money come between our friendship."

"Nothing is coming between our friendship, Mike. We're just making a few extra dollars on the side. If we put our coke together, we will make $75,000, extra! And Eric will still get all of his money."

"I need coke for my strip though," Mike said, scratching his head.

"Yo, Mike, that's 75 G's in ten minutes. It takes our strips about ten days combined to make that kind of money. The strips can wait."

"What about Eric?"

"Eric pays us 5-10 G's a week, depending on what our strips made, and he keeps the majority of the profit. Why should he be making all the money, and we be doing all the work, taking all the risk?"

"But, he put us both in the game when we was two broke nobodies."

"And I'll always love him for that, but it's not '96 no more, times have changed. I got to get all the paper I can get," Larry said.

"I don't know, L, I mean, things is all good right now."

"Can I ask you one question, Mike?"

"What?"

"What are you in this game for?"

Mike remained silent for a moment, as he crossed his arms with his head down, facing the floor. "Okay, Larry. Okay, I'll do it, but we can never let Eric find out about this, so you can't tell nobody else, especially Braheem."

"I won't, don't worry, Mike, everything will be okay. Now you'll be able to make some real paper, and not the same old middle-man allowance we been getting."

With a confused look on his face, Mike looked at Larry.

"Cheer up, Mike, now let's go get our cars washed and shoot out the Plateau, and meet some honeys," Larry said, as he and Mike both stood up and walked out of the apartment.

After dropping Rose and her family off home from church, Eric went home to his apartment where Braheem was there waiting. "What's up, Braheem?" Eric said, walking in the door. "Nothing cuz, I'm just chilling, waiting for you."

"Waiting for me, why? What's up?"

"Today is Sunday, the Plateau, the honeys."

"You're right, Braheem, that's just what it is, Sunday. And from now on just count Eric out. I won't be a part of it anymore," Eric said.

Braheem looked at Eric and smiled. "Just checking. Just checking. So you serious about this girl, huh?"

"As a heart attack."

"I ain't gonna lie, she's worth it, E, that girl is bad. Maybe one day I will meet a shorty like that," Braheem said.

"One thing for sure, you won't meet her out there at the Plateau, ain't nothing out there but vultures. Nothing but Hawks and Vultures," Eric said, as he walked into his bedroom and laid across the bed.

West Park Housing Projects ...

"My God"
"You are the reason why I can live
You are the reason why I can love
My light inside this dark world
Never will I put anything above
When I'm in pain, you're there to heal me

When I'm not understood, you always feel me
When I'm lost, you bring me back
When I run off course, you put me on track
When I'm asleep you bring me dreams
And my dreams turn to peaceful smiles
Forever will you remain my destiny, forever I'll remain your
child
When I'm alone, you're by my side, on this never ending ride
When I'm confused, I can count on you, my love, my hope,
my God."

"That is so pretty," Joyce said, sitting on her couch listening to Rose's poem that she had just written.

"Thank you, Joyce," Rose said. "It's called, 'My God.'"

"So what was it you wanted to talk about, Rose?"

"Eric."

"Eric! So you changed your mind, huh?"

"Yeah, something like that."

"So what's up, talk to me."

"Me and Eric have been seeing each other."

"What! You and Eric. I thought you said …"

"I know, I know, don't remind me, Joyce."

"So you gave in, huh?"

"You can say that. He kinda made it hard to say no."

"So what do you think so far?"

"He's just like you said, Joyce, different."

"I told you. Eric is one of a kind. What I would do to one day meet a man like Eric."

"Guess what," Rose said.

"What?"

"Me and his birthdays are on the same day."

"Your birthday is on the fourth of July too?" Joyce said

91

smiling.

"Yeah, when he told me. I couldn't believe it."

"Ahh man, this is freaking me out. Rose," Joyce said.

"It freaked me out too. That, and he looks so much like my father."

"Maybe it's just meant to be between y'all, who knows. So is it getting serious?" Joyce asked.

"Very. It's scaring me. I wasn't even looking, it just happened so soon."

"Well, that's when things usually happen, when you're not looking."

"I know, it's been tripping me out."

"Like I said, Rose, Eric is a sweetheart. You can't go wrong. I really hope everything turns out right between y'all, I really do," Joyce said.

"How's your eye?"

"It feels better. It's healing good."

"Thank God. I wanted you and your family to go to church with us next Sunday."

"Church!"

"Yeah, what's wrong with church?"

"Nothing, it's just, we haven't been to church in so long."

"I really would love to take y'all to my church and meet my pastor."

"I would love to go. I'll ask my mom. She'll go. Thank you, Rose, for asking me."

"Me and God are going to get you straight," Rose said, putting her arms around Joyce who now had tears rolling down her face.

"Rose, you are truly an angel in disguise."

"Thank you, Joyce, but you are an angel too, no one just ever told you. I'll talk to you later," Rose said, getting up and walking to the door. "And don't forget."

"What?" Joyce said, wiping her tears with her hand. "You are an angel too," Rose said, walking out the door. Laying on his bed asleep, the sound of Eric's cell phone ringing woke him up. "Hello, holla."

"What's up, E. It's me, Keith."

"Yo, what's up, Keith?"

"You money, can I see you tomorrow?"

"What you need?"

"Five chickens for the family. We starving up here in G-town."

"I'll meet you where we always meet, Keith."

"Same time, E?"

"Same time, Keith."

"Same price?"

"Why you ask me the same thing every week. Ain't nothing changed, twenty cents."

"Okay, Eric, I will see you tomorrow," Keith said, hanging up the phone.

Later that night ...

Mike and Larry were in the crib with a beautiful female that they had met at the Belmont Plateau earlier that day. "So what's up sexy," Larry said, as the three of them were all sitting around the large T.V. screen watching an x-rated porn flick.

Standing up, the beautiful 5'5" woman started slowly taking off all of her clothes. Her gorgeous dark brown complexion complemented her hazel eyes and full red lips. Once she was undressed, her luscious hour-glass figure was finally on display, 36-24-38.

"What are y'all waiting for?" she said, looking at Mike and Larry who couldn't believe the perfect ass that they were seeing on this woman. Quickly, they both started getting undressed.

After all three of them were totally naked, the beautiful woman went into the kitchen and walked back out with a chair. "You sit here," she said, pointing to Larry.

He quickly sat down in the chair. "What's up?" he said.

"Just chill, big daddy. I got this," she said, standing up in front of Larry, now telling Mike to come closer behind her. Bending over, she gripped Larry's hard dick with her full red lips and no hands, while slowly swallowing every bit of him. Reaching her arms back, she grabbed Mike by his dick and pulled him closer. Gripping her perfect hips, Mike entered her from behind.

"Awww, ohhh, aaahhh," she moaned, as Mike deeply pen-etrated every inch of himself inside her hairy pink pussy. After both men came, they quickly switched positions. Now stand-ing behind her, while she sucked on Mike's dick, Larry entered her from behind. "Ohhh, ahhh, awww," she moaned, as she couldn't control the multiple orgasms that her body was now feeling.

For the remainder of the night, Mike and Larry both enjoyed the sexual pleasures of this beautiful woman. And at the same time, she was enjoying both of them.

Chapter Eleven

Monday evening...

Eric, Braheem, Mike and Larry stood around in the kitchen of the crib talking. Forty kilos of cocaine sat around, wrapped on the table and floor. A digital scale was also on the table, with $200,000 in cash. In a chair were two brand new bullet proof vests and a chrome 380 handgun. In another chair were five pounds of marijuana inside a green trash bag.

"Get your ten, Mike," Eric said, pointing at the cocaine on the table.

Mike began putting the kilos inside a black sports bag that was on his shoulders.

"That's yours, Braheem," Eric said, pointing to the green trash bag full of hydroweed. "Take fifteen, Larry."

Larry quickly began putting fifteen kilos inside a black sports bag he had. "Slow down, Larry, why you in a rush?" Braheem said.

"What's up with one of those vests, E?" Larry said. "I need one of them."

"Take one."

"Can I get one, Eric?" Mike asked.

"Yeah, go head."

"What's up with that burner?" Braheem asked.

"Ain't nothing up. That's mine. It's brand new straight out the box."

"You already got a hammer," Eric said.

"Ain't nothing ever wrong with another hammer," Braheem said smiling.

"All right, fellows, watch y'all self," Eric said walking into the living room.

One at a time, each person grabbed his bag and walked out the door. Eric stood in the doorway until each of them drove away. Once they had left, he walked back inside and shut the door.

Pulling out his cell phone, he began dialing a number.

"Hello, a voice said answering the phone.

"What's up? You ready?"

"Yeah, I've been waiting."

"Okay, I'll see you in one hour. It's 7:35, so 8:30 you know where to meet me."

"I'll be there waiting."

"Peace." Eric said, hanging up his phone.

Eric then put the last 15 kilos inside a trash bag and grabbed the chrome 380 hand gun off the chair.

After turning off all the lights inside the apartment, he turned on the T.V. in the living room and hurried out the door.

An hour later...

Pulling into the McDonald's parking lot on Broad and Diamond Streets in north Philly. Eric noticed the convertible CL500 Mercedes Benz parked and Keith sitting inside all alone.

As he parked next to him, Keith quickly got out of his car and into Eric's holding a brown bag.

"What's up, E?"

"What's up, Keith, is it all there?"

"Yeah, $100,000."

"It's on the back seat," Eric said pointing to a brown bag he had sitting on the back seat with five kilos neatly packed inside of it.

"Who's them?" Eric said, looking at the two guys getting into Keith's car.

"Oh, them my two homies," Keith said as he shook Eric's hand and quickly got out of the car. "Them two niggas got my back, I don't do nothing without them. Same time next week, E?" Keith said.

"Call me," Eric said, pulling out of the crowded parking lot and driving down Broad Street.

Keith then got into his car where his two friends were both waiting. He then drove off also.

Thirty minutes later...

Rose was downstairs waiting in the doorway when Eric pulled up into the project's parking lot. Walking to the car, she got inside.

"Hey, baby," Rose said, leaning over kissing Eric on his lips.

"I got something for you pretty," Eric said, getting out of his car and going into his trunk. He then got back inside his car holding a small white bag.

"Here," Eric said handing her the bag with a box inside of it.

"What's this, Eric?" Rose asked smiling.

"Look in and see," Eric smiled back.

Opening up the bag, Rose pulled out the small box. "Eric, what is it?"

"Just open it and see for yourself."

Opening up the box, both of Rose's eyes lit up as she stared at the pair of diamond studded earrings that Eric had bought her. "Oh, Eric, they are so beautiful! Oh, my God, Eric, thank you," Rose said leaning over and giving him another kiss.

"Put them on," Eric said.

"Right now? But I'm going to work?"

"Right now, I want to see them in your ears everyday from now on."

Taking them from the box, Rose put them both in her ears. "How do they look?" she asked, looking at Eric smiling.

"Beautiful, just like you," He said backing up and pulling off.

Tuesday afternoon...

At Mario's uncle's garage in south Philly, Mario, Vinny, Larry and Mike were all in the back room. Sitting on a table was a briefcase with $500,000 in cash inside. On the floor next to Larry were 25 kilos of cocaine inside a large trash bag. With his 9 mm handgun on his hip, Mike stood nervously by the door, looking out the window for anything suspicious.

Mario then passed Larry the briefcase. "Go ahead, count it. It's all there," he confidently said.

Larry began counting the money. After counting the money, he shook his head at Mike. "Okay, fellas, here's your 25 birds," Larry said, folding the briefcase up and walking towards the door.

"I'll call you, L," Mario said.

"Okay, Mario. Okay, Vinny. I'll see y'all," he said as he and Mike walked out the door.

Getting back into his car. Larry and Mike quickly pulled off.

"Ten minutes, like I told you. the fastest $75,000 you ever made in your whole life," Larry smilingly said.

"Man, that *was* quick," Mike said.

"I told you. this is where the moneys at, selling weight. Fuck them drug strips."

Mike just shook his head looking inside the briefcase at the money.

"Man, a half million dollars is sitting on my lap."

"Yeah, and $425,000 is Eric's," Larry said with an uneasy look on his face.

Saturday morning — four days later...

At the West Park Housing Projects. Eric knocked on the door once, then he walked inside of the quiet apartment.

"Hey, Ms. Joann," Eric said, walking into the kitchen.

"Hey, Eric. I didn't hear you come in," she said, giving him a warm hug. "How's your mother doing?"

"She's doing okay. Hey y'all," Eric said. kissing Brandy and Aiesha, who were sitting at the table eating their bowls of cereal.

"Where's Joyce?"

"She's in her bedroom sleeping with Ryan," Ms. Joann said. "Go wake her up. She's been sleeping all morning. It's 11 o'clock. She should have been up."

Eric walked into Joyce's room as she slept under the covers with Ryan next to her. Eric sat on the foot of her bed.

Taping Joyce on the feet, Eric woke her up from her sleep. Taking the covers from off of her head, Eric noticed her bruised eye. "What happened to you? How did that happen!?"

"Nothing. I fell at work. It's nothing, Eric."

"That don't look like you fell, Joyce, don't lie to me, what happened?"

"Eric, I told you, I fell, now leave it alone please."

"No, not until you tell me what really happened to your eye," Eric demanded.

"I told you, I fell. Please, Eric, just let it go."

"Joyce, if somebody put their hands on you, you better tell me."

"Ain't nobody touched me, Eric, now please just leave it alone."

"Okay, Joyce, but if somebody put their hands on you and you ain't telling me, I'm going to be very upset when I do find out. And I will find out."

"Eric, please, just leave it alone," Joyce said as Eric got up off the bed and walked back into the kitchen.

Reaching into his pocket, he pulled out five $100 bills and gave them to Ms. Joann. After kissing the girls on the cheeks, he sadly walked out the door.

Walking up the stairs to Rose's apartment, Eric knocked on the door. Looking out the peephole, Rose saw that it was Eric and quickly opened up the door.

"Hey, baby, why didn't you tell me that you were coming by?"

"I went to see Ms. Joann and Joyce."

"You saw Joyce?" Rose said in a shocked voice.

"Yeah! Do you know what happened to her eye?" Eric asked.

"Eric, please don't get me involved with y'all business."

"If somebody put their hands on her, I want to know. Do you know what happened, Rose?"

"Eric, she told me not to tell you."

"Rose, if you know what happened, please tell me."

"Eric, I promised her I wouldn't say anything."

"You also promised me you would never keep anything away from me."

"But I was talking about me and your business."

"Rose, Joyce and her family are my business. Anything happens to them affects me. Please tell me what happened to her."

"She was raped, Eric! Joyce was raped! Are you satisfied, now you know?"

"What! Who raped her? When did this happen?"

"Last week. She was gang raped by three guys."

"Why didn't anybody tell me? How could you keep this away from me?"

"Joyce was afraid. She didn't want you to find out. She was afraid of what you would do. She was worried about you and how much you had to lose."

"I don't care about none of that. She's like my little sister. How do you think I feel? I've known her all my life. Who did it? Tell me who did it," Eric yelled.

"I don't know. She didn't say too much. She just mentioned some guy named Keith."

"That's it? That's all she knows is Keith?"

"He drives a platinum convertible Mercedes Benz, and he lives in Germantown."

"What! What did you say?" Eric said, taking a seat on the sofa.

"His name is Keith and he drives a convertible Mercedes Benz."

"Thank you." Eric said running out the door.

"Eric, Eric," Rose said, running behind him.

But it was too late. Eric was already halfway down the stairs.

Walking downstairs, Rose met Joyce in the hallway who was on her way up to see her.

"I'm sorry. Joyce, but he wouldn't stop asking until he got an answer."

"I don't blame you, Rose. I know how Eric can get. He has a way of making people do or say things that they don't want to sometimes."

"I hope he don't do anything stupid," Rose said.

"Eric knows these streets and the people who live on these streets, he has a reputation about the way he operates. He wouldn't do nothing stupid."

"I hope so. Sometimes people can get so sidetracked that they forget to think straight."

"Maybe he will calm down. He's just a little upset," Joyce said, walking to her front door.

"Yeah, maybe he'll calm down and realize that what's done is done," Rose said walking upstairs to her apartment.

Later that evening, driving in his car with Braheem and Mike, Eric called Rose from his cell phone.

Sitting on her bed writing a poem, Rose picked up the phone. "Hello."

"What's up baby?"

"Hey Eric, are you okay? I was worried about you."

"I'm fine. I just had to go for a ride and calm down."

"I'm sorry I didn't tell you, but Joyce was afraid and she had asked me not to tell anyone. She even told Ms. Joann that it happened at work also so she wouldn't be worried either."

"I understand. I shouldn't have forced you to tell me. Do you accept my apology?"

"Yes, Eric. I accept your apology," Rose smilingly said.

"Thank you baby. I'll be there in a little while to take you to work."

"Okay," Rose said. "Bye Eric."

"Bye, Rose," Eric said, closing up his cell phone.

Rose then called Joyce on the phone. "Hello," Joyce answered.

"Joyce, it's me, Rose."

"Hey, Rose, what's up?"

"I just got off the phone with Eric."

"Is he okay? Is everything all right?"

"Yeah. He just needed to calm down. He was just hurt, that's all."

"I'm glad. My mom said that he had called. I had gone out to the grocery store," Joyce said.

"That boy really loves you, Joyce," Rose said.

"He loves my whole family. Ever since my dad went to jail and asked him to look out for us, he's been like that. Him and my father were very close. Eric never knew his own father, but he was real close to my father when he was young."

"Now I see why he's so overprotective about you and your family."

"Yeah, he's like our big brother, even though I had grown up always having a crush on Eric. He just always looked at me as nothing more than a little sister."

"I had written a poem for you, Joyce, that's why I called."

"For me? Can I hear it?"

"Yeah, one moment," Rose said, picking up her white pad.

Sitting straight up on her bed, Rose began reading it over the phone.

"What is it called?" Joyce asked. *"The Daisy That Grew From Dirt."* "Okay, go ahead. I'm ready." Joyce said.

"How can someone else know me if I don't even know myself?

Why do we judge love on materialistic items, and others fading wealth?

The ghetto makes us cry without tears, grow older by the years.

But no one ever said that this life we live in was fair.

I call myself a woman, but often I think like a young girl.

I'm the main reason for my own heartache, but I blame it on this cruel world.

I'm a victim inside this nightmare looking to escape.

Before my body was violated, my spirituality was raped.

Still, I'm a mother, a sister, a queen on God's earth.

And no matter how many times I'm stepped on, I'm still that daisy who grew from dirt."

"So just remember, Joyce, no matter what, you are still a *Flower*. Did you like it? Hello. Hello," Rose said. "Joyce."

"Yes, Rose, I loved it. I loved it a lot," Joyce tearfully said. "It was very beautiful. Thank you so much for sharing it with me. Thank you so much, Rose. Can I please have that poem?"

"Yes, you can have it, Joyce, it's yours."

"Thank you," Joyce said as the tears ran down her face. "Thank you, Rose."

For the next few days, everything seemed to get back to the norm. Eric would take Rose back and forth to work, always surprising Rose with a gift every time he would pick her up.

Rose and Joyce's families went to church together where Joyce even decided to give herself to the Lord and get baptized.

Braheem, Mike and Larry couldn't stay away from their favorite weekend hangout, the Belmont Plateau where beautiful women and luxury cars were always waiting.

Eric and Rose's relationship became more and more serious, each realizing that they both played very important parts in each other's life. Eric even decided to tell all his other female friends that he was no longer a single man, breaking many hearts all throughout the city. But he knew Rose was worth it all.

As for Braheem, Mike and Larry, life couldn't get any better. Each had all they could ever wish for. Money, cars, jewelry, women. Every day to them was like an adventure – a non-stop party.

This is what they had all envisioned two years ago when Eric first put this young team together, when Eric laid his blueprint down and told each one of them the rules of the game and the roles that everyone would play by.

Eric had 10 rules that he called the **Rules of the game**, promising everyone if they followed these 10 simple rules, nothing could ever stop them.

Loyalty – never cross the family.

Trust – always have each other's back.

Respect – always give respect the way you want to be respected.

Roles – everyone has a role to play; no one is more important than the other.

Decisions – think before you react. Making the right decisions are very important.

Women – never let a woman come between the family. Love, but don't lust.

Family – everything we do is to better our families and loved ones. Family is our strength.

No jealousy – a jealous man has an evil heart and an evil heart can destroy a kingdom.

Drugs – never, ever do drugs ... period.

Twenty-five – if you follow rules 1 through 9, by the age of

25, we'll all be young millionaires.

Chapter Twelve

9 p.m. Monday night ...

The McDonald's parking lot was crowded as normal on this chilly night. Keith and his friend saw Eric when he pulled up and parked at the opposite end of the large parking lot.

Getting out of his Benz, Keith was holding a small brown bag while his two friends remained sitting inside listening to the radio that was playing.

Eric unlocked his door as Keith approached the car and got inside.

"What's up, E?"

"Same ol, same ol, business as usual," Eric said.

"Here you go." Keith said, passing Eric the brown bag.

Opening it up and looking inside, Eric saw the bundles of neatly stacked money inside.

"One-hundred thousand. You can count it, it's all there."

"I trust you, backseat," Eric said, pointing to the backseat where a brown bag was sitting.

"Same stuff, E?" Keith asked, grabbing the bag from the seat.

"Same stuff, Keith, 5 keez."

"Okay, I'll see you next week, E," Keith said getting out of the car holding the brown bag in his arms.

Eric remained sitting until Keith had gotten inside his car. As Keith started up his engine and was ready to pull off, a brown Dodge Caravan quickly pulled in front of him, blocking him from driving off.

Before Keith and his two friends realized what was happening, the side door of the van quickly swung open and two masked gunmen, one armed with an 1100 semiautomatic 12-gauge shotgun, and the other holding two black Berretta 9 mm's, jumped out and started to unload every single bullet into Keith's Mercedes.

People began running as the screams started filling the air. Once the two masked gunmen jumped back into the van, the driver quickly pulled off, driving down the crowded Broad Street, blending in with the moving traffic.

A few moments later, Eric got out of his car and walked up to the small crowd that now was gathered around the mangled Mercedes Benz and its three dead passengers. Looking on, Eric could see the devastation that the guns had done. Hearing the sirens of police cars fastly approaching, Eric then walked back to his car, got in and drove away.

Driving down Broad Street, Eric called Rose on his cell phone.

"Hello," Rose said answering the phone.

"What's up baby? I'm on my way. I'll be there in about a half hour." Eric said.

"How was your day, Eric?"

"Today was a good day. Everything went well."

"Okay, baby, let me hurry up and get dressed. I'll be waiting outside when you pull up. Bye," Rose said.

"Bye," Eric said closing up his cell phone.

After Eric dropped Rose off at work, he immediately drove

to the crib in southwest Philly where Braheem, Mike and Larry were all waiting for him.

Entering the apartment, the three of them were all sitting in the living room playing the Sony Playstation video game.

"What's up, fellas?" Eric said taking a seat on the couch.

"We been waiting for you. What took you so long?" Braheem said.

"Business," Eric said. "Always got to make sure business is taken care of right."

Going into a back room, Eric walked out with a trash bag full of kilos of cocaine.

"Time to take care of our B-I," Eric said sitting back down.

Emptying out the large bag onto the carpet, Eric began to pass to each one his weekly work.

Joyce was laying on her bed with the T.V. on while Ryan was asleep next to her. Getting under her blanket, Joyce grabbed the remote control from off of her night table, and turned on Channel 10's 11 o'clock Nightly News that was just coming on.

A news reporter, who was live at the tragic scene, began to tell of the story.

*"**Earlier tonight**, at this popular McDonald's restaurant on the corner of Broad and Diamond Streets in north Philadelphia, three men were tragically gunned down, executioner style, inside of this 1998 convertible Mercedes Benz. Witnesses on the scene said two masked men with semiautomatic weapons jumped out of a van and began shooting the three victims in this brutal assassination. The victims, Keith Morgan, Omar Longtree and Kalvin Ralley, all from Philadelphia, were all dead on the scene moments before the Philadelphia police arrived.*

"The Philadelphia Homicide Unit is now on the scene searching

for clues. The only clue so far is a brown bag containing five kilograms of flour. Detectives on the police force believe that it was a drug deal gone wrong, one of many that's been the cause of so many deaths in Philadelphia's war on drugs.

"Any information on this case, please contact the Philadelphia Homicide Unit at 685-H-E-L-P-L-A-W."

Joyce turned off her T.V. and laid back under the blanket. "Eric," she said, smiling to herself, and shaking her head. "I know Eric had something to do with it," she said as she then closed her eyes and peacefully fell asleep.

Tuesday afternoon, West Park Housing Projects. . .

Eric knocked on the door once, then walked inside the apartment. Joyce and Ms. Joann were sitting at the kitchen table talking. "Eric, hey baby," Ms. Joann said, giving him a big hug.

"Hi, Eric, what's that?" Joyce said, pointing at a white sneaker bag that Eric had in his hands.

"This is y'alls," he said, dumping the bag out on the table.

Ms. Joann and Joyce's eyes both lit up seeing all the hundred and fifty dollar bills scattered on the kitchen table.

"This is yours, Ms. Joann, it's for you and your family. Please don't ask me any questions, just take it."

Tears began to fall down Ms. Joann and Joyce's eyes.

"Thank you, Eric, so much. I don't know what to say. I just can't believe it," Ms. Joann said nervously shaking.

"How much is it?" Joyce asked, picking up a large stack of hundreds.

"It's $100,000."

"Ms. Joann, I want you and the girls to move, move as soon as possible. There's enough money to buy you a nice little house and even a car. Can you please do that, Ms. Joann?" Eric asked.

"Yes, Eric, I will. I'll buy a paper today and start looking for a nice house. Thank you so much, Eric. Thank you so much," she said, putting the money back into the white sneaker bag.

"Joyce, do you got a minute?" Eric said, walking into her bedroom.

"Yeah, Eric," Joyce said, following closely behind him.

Eric sat on the bed as Joyce shut the door and sat beside him with a big smile on her face.

"I saw the news last night, Eric," Joyce said.

"You did?"

"Yeah. Thank you."

Eric didn't say a word, he just looked at Joyce and they both smiled together.

"Joyce, I want you and your mom to do the right thing with that money. Promise me you'll start getting your life straight."

"I promise, Eric. I been going to church with Rose. She's really been supportive and a real good friend."

"I want your family to get out of these dangerous projects."

"We can now, thanks to you, Eric," Joyce said smiling.

"You know I love you, right, lil sis?"

"I know, Eric," Joyce said as the tears began to roll down her face.

"How does your eye feel?"

"It feels better. I'm alright, Eric, I don't know what me and my family would ever do without you."

"Don't worry about me, Joyce. I'll be okay. You just make sure you and your family are all right. And get as far away from these projects as y'all can."

"We will. We will be out in two weeks, I promise."

"Here," Eric said, passing Joyce a key that was in his hand.

"What's this for?"

"It's for you. It's to my apartment. If you can't never get in touch with me and something like this ever happened again, or anything, you go to my apartment, and wait for me."

"I will, Eric," Joyce said taking the key.

Eric then reached over and hugged Joyce. "If anything ever happens to you like that again, you better let me know."

"I will, I promise. Thank you, Eric. Thank you so much for being there for me and my family."

"You're welcome, lil sis. I know you would have done the same for me."

"This is the happiest day of my life," Joyce said.

"And mine too," Eric said. "Mine too."

Two weeks later ...

Joyce and her family moved into a four-bedroom, two-story house in southwest Philly, a few blocks away from Eric's mother's house. Joyce also bought a 1997 Ford Taurus that she would use to drop her little sisters off to school in and also take her and Rose to their job at the post office.

Finally, the dangerous environment of the projects was behind them and life was beginning to look so much better with Joyce and her family.

Larry and Mike had become partners and now were selling 25 kilos a week to Mario and Vinny.

The murders of Keith and his friends had baffled the police, who still had very little clues to go on. And not one suspect arrested.

Friday night...

Mike and Braheem both waited while Eric went inside the house on 6th and Erie Avenue holding a black briefcase in his hand.

Inside, two Dominican men were sitting at a large round table while another guy was standing by the door holding a Teck-nine-semiautomatic machine gun.

"One minute," one of the men said to Eric, running into the back room. Moments later, he and another man came out.

"Thank you, Raul," the man said sitting down.

"Eric, Eric, my friend, I see I don't ever have to call you."

"What's up, Jose?" Eric said.

"You, my young friend. I see business has been good."

"Business has been great. I can't complain."

"Eric, for you, I would do anything. You make me very proud and rich," Jose said smiling. "What do you have for me, my friend?" Jose said, looking at the briefcase.

Opening up the briefcase, Eric laid it on the table and took a step back. "A million dollars," he said.

"So business has been great, huh?" Jose said smiling.

"Nino, Romero, go get that," Jose said to the two men who were sitting at the table.

Nino and Romero both ran to the back room, then came back out, each holding a large black Hefty trash bag. "There's twenty-five keys in each bag, Eric. I guess I'll see you next week, huh?"

"You should, Jose, no longer than two," Eric said, walking to the door. "Oh yeah, thank you for taking care of that problem."

"No problem, my friend. For you, anything," Jose said.

Nino and Romero both followed Eric outside to his car

who put the two large bags inside the trunk.

Eric then pulled off with Mike and Braheem closely behind him.

Thirty minutes later...

Larry was outside the crib waiting when both cars pulled into the driveway. Grabbing both bags from the trunk, Mike and Braheem followed Eric and Larry into the apartment.

"Y'alls are in that bag," Eric said to Mike. "Your 10 and Larry's 15. Braheem, put that bag up," Eric said taking a seat.

Braheem walked into a back room with the other bag in his hand. "Y'all two have been doing good. Y'all both stepped up y'all games. I told y'all if you concentrate on this paper, like y'all do them girls, y'all would both be millionaires by 25."

"You was right, E. Nothing is more important than this paper," Larry said, looking at Mike.

Braheem then walked out from the back room and sat down next to Eric.

"I'm proud of y'all, my two brothers," Eric said smiling.

"As long as we stay tight like this, life will be lovely."

"Never forget that we make paper; paper don't make us."

"And never forget the 10 rules and we will all be millionaires," Eric said.

Mike and Larry both walked to the door.

"E, I'll call you later," Larry said rushing out the door.

"What's wrong, Mike," Eric asked.

"Nothing. I was just thinking about something, that's all. I'll talk to you later, E," Mike said, walking out the door holding the large bag over his shoulder.

"Make sure everything is cool, Braheem," Eric said as he turned on the T.V.

Braheem then followed Mike and Larry outside to Larry's car. When they had driven off, he came back inside.

"Mike don't seem the same."

"I think something is on his mind too," Eric said.

"He's been that way for the last few weeks," Braheem said, sitting on the couch next to Eric.

"I think he wants to tell me something. I know Mike, I know when something ain't right with him. What do you think it is, Braheem?"

"Probably some girl," Braheem said, as he started laughing out loud. Eric didn't laugh. He knew something just wasn't right with his best friend.

Chapter Thirteen

Saturday night...

Rose and Eric were both sitting in his Infiniti outside of the projects talking. Rose had just gotten off work and both had something special to tell each other.

"What is it? What's so important?" Rose said.

"You tell me first," Eric said smiling.

"I'm going to quit stripping. Next week is my last week. I'm through. I know you don't like me doing it, and I thank you for not tripping and letting me stop on my own. I already told my boss that next week will be my last time there."

Reaching over, kissing her, he said, "I'm proud of you, Rose."

"Now, what is it that you wanted to tell me?"

"A few days ago I went by your school."

"Temple!" Rose said in a shocking voice.

"Yeah. I have a good friend who works down there, in the student finance department. He called me today and said he's looking forward to seeing you back there starting the winter semester."

"What are you talking about, Eric?"

"You heard me. You're going to finish college and get your degree."

"But I don't have the money. I can't afford it right now."

"It's all paid for. You don't have to pay for nothing, not even your books."

"Eric, tell me you are joking," Rose said looking him in his eyes.

"I'm serious as a heart attack. We got to get you that degree."

"Thank you, Eric. I don't know what to say," Rose said with tears falling down her face as she and Eric embraced in a long emotional hug. "Thank you so much," she said.

Sunday evening...

Inside the crib, Mike and Larry were sitting on the couch. "So why didn't you want to go to the Belmont Plateau today?" Larry asked.

"I just didn't feel like it, Larry."

"What's wrong with you, Mike?"

"I can't do it no more, Larry," Mike said.

"Can't do what? Man, don't start flippin' on me."

"I can't mess with Mario and Vinny no more. I don't care about the money. Everything I got, I got from dealing with Eric, my car, my apartment, all he ever did was show me love. I owe him my loyalty."

"How can you back out now? How can you not want extra money?"

"Eric said something and when he said it, I realize it's not about the money, but the respect. He said, *'Paper don't make us; we make the paper.'* All I've been worried about is my own greed. For a few more dollars, I been playing myself. The money we make is more than enough. We have a tight click, nothing should be more important than that. Nothing is more important than the 10 rules."

"So you're going to back out on me now?" an angry Larry said.

"Next time will be my last time serving them. You can go head. I don't want no more parts of it. I don't want their money."

"But how will I be able to supply them their 25 keys every week?"

"I don't know. Ask Eric for more."

"But he will know something ain't right then."

"Then you should leave it alone before he finds out we went behind his back."

"Come on, Mike," Larry begged.

"No, Larry, that's it, next week is it for me," Mike said walking out of the apartment leaving Larry by himself.

Later that evening...

"So you like your new house, Brandy?" Rose said talking to Joyce's younger sister on the telephone.

"Yes, Rose. I got my own room. Sometimes I still sleep with Aiesha. Here go Joyce now," Brandy said, passing the phone to Joyce.

"What's up girl?" Joyce said in a cheerful tone.

"Did you enjoy church today?"

"Yes, I did. Church was wonderful. Now tell me the good news and stop beating around the bush."

"I'm going back to college."

"What? When?"

"Once the winter semester begins. Eric paid for my remaining two years."

"Oh, Rose, I'm so happy for you. I know how much you wanted to finish your college education and get your degree."

"You were right, Joyce. Eric *is* different. He is a wonderful man."

"I told you. I told you. Ain't too many men like Eric."

"I'm really beginning to believe that."

"Rose, can I ask you something?"

"Go ahead."

"Do you love Eric?"

"Why do you ask me that?"

"I just never heard you say it."

"Yes, Joyce, I love Eric. I love Eric very much."

"Did you ever tell him?"

"No, not yet."

"What are you waiting for?"

"The only man I ever told that I love was my father. I know that he would never break my heart, that he wouldn't take those three words and run with them. I'm just afraid to tell Eric how much I'm in love with him and how much I truly care for him."

"Do you think he loves you?"

"Yes, I think he loves me, and I think he feels the same way as I do and he don't know how to tell me either. Every time we are together, there is a chemistry between us that I just can't describe, just can't explain. I'm just afraid, Joyce."

"Afraid of what, Rose?"

"I'm afraid of his lifestyle. I'm afraid of losing him to the streets. I'm afraid of going through the pain of losing the most important person in my life, once again."

"Well, did you tell him that?"

"No, that's something a man must decide on his own. Walking away from the streets is the hardest thing to do for any hustler. My father tried, but he just couldn't do it, and all it got him was life. If I ever lost Eric, I would be devastated."

"Well, I think you're doing the right thing. Once he sees that the streets ain't worth it, he'll come around, he will change."

"I hope so, Joyce, I really hope so. I pray for it every day. I ask God to watch over Eric and keep him safe on those streets. Those streets are nothing but the devil, and sometimes we can't see through his evil ways, his deceitful intentions, sometimes he's right under our nose and we never know it. And once we realize he was playing us the whole time it's too late."

"You're right about that, Rose. You are so right. I had to learn the hard way," Joyce said. "Sometimes he's right under our nose, and we never even know it."

Monday morning...

At the post office, Rose and Joyce were sitting at their counters separating the large piles of mail in front of them.

"Joyce?"

"Yes, Rose."

"How does a woman know when she's ready?"

"Ready? Ready for what?"

"Ready, Joyce, you know what I mean."

"When all you do is eat, drink and sleep that somebody, when every moment without him is a minute too long, when every time you're around him, you could just tear his clothes off, when all you do is dream and fantasize about him, when your mind has no more control and your body has given in, you'll know when you're ready. You will say, '*This is what I want and I got to have it*,'" Joyce said as they both began smiling.

That afternoon at the North American Motel, City Line Avenue ...

Larry and a female friend were both laying across the bed naked. Hearing his cell phone ring, Larry reached over and answered it.

"Hello," he said answering his phone while playing with the female's breast.

"Yo, L, it's me, Mario."

"Yo, what's up. I been waiting to hear from you. Are you ready?"

"No, Friday I'll be ready. Friday, me and Vinny should be finished."

"Okay, that's fine. What do y'all need?"

"A bucket of chicken from Kentucky Fried."

"How many pieces?"

"Twenty-five," Mario said.

"No problem. I'll see y'all Friday," Larry said closing up his cell phone. "Now, back to you," he said looking at the Pamela Anderson look-a-like.

"Who was that?" she said snorting a straw full of coke up her nose.

"That was your brother."

"Mario?" she said enjoying the instant rush.

"Yeah, Mario."

"I told you that y'all could do some good business together," she said, passing the straw and small mirror filled with cocaine on it to Larry.

After taking a long snort, Larry sat back against the bed-post. "Yeah, you was right, Bunny. I'm making a lot of money with your brother," Larry said, as he laid the straw and mirror back on the dresser.

"Baby, can I have some now, please, can I have some of that big black long dick of yours?"

"Come here," Larry said, pushing the blankets off the bed. "Do you love this big dick? Do daddy fuck you right?"

"Yes," Bunny said getting on top of Larry. "Yes, yes, I love this dick, I love this big black dick," she said as she began riding Larry like a brand new Porsche.

Inside the Platinum Club, in a private room, Mario, Vinny and two men were talking. "Everything is going perfect. Bunny got the mooley wrapped around her fingers," Mario said smiling at Vinny.

"She deserves a bonus for this one," Vinny said.

"You sure the nigger don't know what's going on?" one of the men said.

"Uncle Perotta, this guy only thinks about hisself and his dick. He was the right person to sick Bunny on at the club," Mario said. "Friday, he's bringing 25 keys to the garage. That's where we will kidnap him and his friend and find a place for them in the Schuylkill River.

"Make sure your hands are clean."

"Unc, don't we always?" Mario said smiling.

"He trusts us. He has no idea that it will be a set up. He's only worried about the $500,000 geez that he's not getting," Vinny said.

"All them mooleys do is think with their dicks and listen to that fucking rap music," Mario said as they all started laughing.

Later that evening...

Sitting at a table inside the Caribbean Delight Restaurant on 11th and South Street, Eric, Braheem and Larry were talking and eating.

"I want us to start doing the right thing with our cash," Eric said.

"Like what?" Braheem said eating his bowl of curried chicken.

"Property, investments. I want all of us to be set for the rest of our lives and all of our families' as well.

"What do you think, Mike?"

"Mike, hey Mike, wake up and stop daydreaming," Eric said bringing Mike back to the scene.

"What's been wrong with you, Mike? For three weeks you been on cloud nine."

"Cloud 99," Braheem sarcastically said.

"You're my best friend. You know you could tell me anything. What's wrong?"

"Nothing E. I just been having some things on my mind. I just been thinking I want to start investing too, you know like me that this shit don't last."

"That's what I'm saying. I was thinking about opening up a few daycares, all around the city, only charging a few dollars for women who can't afford the expensive daycare's prices."

"You mean for women in the projects?" Braheem said.

"Exactly. Women who're struggling every day with three and four kids and wouldn't have a problem paying a small fee."

"That sounds like a good idea, Eric," Mike said. "I'm ready to change my life anyway. I'm really getting tired of the game."

"Is that what's been on your mind, Mike?" Eric asked.

"Yeah. That and those guys at the McDonald's."

"What about them niggas?" Braheem said.

"Ever since that day, I thought about us. Just like them, that could have been us getting hit up. How tomorrow is never guaranteed. They had money, cars, and everything we got. Now just like that, they're dead. I think about how things will turn out all the time. I pray that we can get out of this game alive. Everybody we know is either dead or in prison doing time."

"**Mark, Man, Troy** and **Rob** are no longer with us now because of some haters and this back stabbing game. And look at **Jimmy, Duke** and **Almoney**, all in the feds serving decades. That's what's been on my mind, Eric, getting out of this game and one day hopefully raising a family."

"We will, Mike. We're all gonna make it out," Eric said, putting his arms around his best friend.

"Now, eat your food and stop stressing, man, if we all stick to the 10 rules, nothing will stop us."

Chapter Fourteen

Tuesday evening...

Rose was sitting on the sofa watching T.V. with her two little brothers. Hearing the phone ring, Rose picked it up and answered.

"Hello," Rose said.

After a few seconds, a voice recorder spoke. "This is a prepaid call. You will not be charged for this call. This call is from *Johnny Ray*. To accept this phone call, dial five now. To cancel this phone call and any other calls from this person, press 77." Rose quickly pressed five.

"Daddy! Daddy! I'm sorry I missed your call the other day. Mommy told me that you called. How are you doing, Daddy?"

"I'm fine, sweetheart. Where's your mom?"

"She's asleep. Do you want me to go wake her up?"

"No. No. I wanted to talk to you anyway, beautiful."

"What's up Daddy?"

"Your mother said you had some good news to tell me. What is it?"

"Oh, I'm going back to college. I start in September."

"Baby, that's wonderful. How did you manage that?"

"It wasn't me, Daddy, it was Eric. Eric did it for me."

"Eric. How did he do it?"

"He has a friend at my school and he paid off all of my remaining two years. Eric did it for me. He told me nothing is more important than my degree."

"Baby, you tell Eric I said thank you."

"I will. I promise."

"It sounds like my baby girl is in love. Is Eric taking you away from me?"

"Daddy, no man can ever replace you. Stop that."

"Well, honey, someday, someone will come and take you away."

"How will I ever know when that day is here?"

"You will have a feeling in your heart, a feeling that you never felt before, when your heart tells you it's real. Do you love Eric, Rose?"

"I think so Daddy. Yes, I think I do."

"Does he know?"

"I'm not sure. I never told him before."

"Did he tell you?"

"No, we never bring it up. Daddy, ever since I was a little girl, you told me to never tell a man I love him before he tells me. And if I'm not 100 percent sure of myself, and how I truly feel to never lie to him. And that the word love was never to be played with."

"You remembered," Johnny Ray said smiling.

"Yes, I remember. I remember everything that you ever told me and everything you ever showed me. How you would sit me down on your lap when I was a little girl and tell me that I was your little queen. And once I got older, it was you, Daddy, who said to never be less than a queen. It was you who told me that life is like a chess game, every piece must know their part. The pawns are responsible soldiers, and the knights and bishops are your fighters, your warriors. How the rooks protect your kingdom, but the queen was always the most dominant piece on the board, and that you were my king. And the queen always protected her king. Daddy, you're my king and you'll always be my king. No one could ever take that title away from you," Rose said.

"Baby, I got to go now," Johnny Ray said, hearing the phone beeping to signify it was about to disconnect. "I love you, my Rose. Tell your brothers and mother I'll call 'em soon."

"Okay, Daddy, I will, and I love you too," Rose said as the phones disconnected.

Later that evening...

Mike and Braheem sat in the living room of the crib counting money. "How much is that, Braheem?" Mike said, pointing to the large stack of money all piled on the floor next to his feet.

"One-hundred thousand! Each stack is $100,000," Braheem said, pointing at the other two stacks of money that were on top of the glass coffee table.

"Where's Larry? He's supposed to be here counting too," Braheem said.

"Probably out tricking as usual."

"I don't know why Eric deals with him. Sometimes he acts like he ain't even down."

"That's Eric's high school buddy. They were real tight back in school when they played on the Overbrook basketball team together."

"Still, he should be here counting with us," Braheem said as he put another stack of money into another large pile.

"Hey, if Eric don't say nothing, we can't say nothing. That's not our job to baby sit Larry. Eric knows him better than all of us. He will handle him."

The phone rang and Braheem picked it up.

"Hello?" he answered and began listening to the person on the other line.

"Yeah. Yeah. Okay, All right, I'll see you." Braheem said hanging up the phone.

"Who was that?"

"That was Larry."

"What he say?" Mike said.

"He asked was you here, then he asked did we start yet. Then he said he was dropping off his Bunny. Then he said he would be here soon."

They just both burst out laughing and finished counting the rest of the money.

Ten o'clock that night. . .

Rose and two other girls were all waiting outside by the side door of the Platinum Club. Moments later, Eric pulled up at the door in his Infiniti.

"Hey, baby, you ready to go?" Eric said.

Walking over to the car, "Eric, could you drop my friends off?" Rose politely asked.

"Yeah, tell them to come on."

Pulling up behind Eric, a white Range Rover truck parked.

"Oh, never mind. That's Bunny's ride. She's okay. We can just drop Coffee off at home."

"Come on, Coffee, get in," Rose said.

After Coffee got inside the car, Eric drove off.

"She lives on 23rd and Tasker in south Philly," Rose said smiling.

"Why are you so happy tonight and how did you get off so early?"

"I feel good, that's why I'm happy. And I asked my boss could I get off early and he said yes."

"So your feet don't hurt tonight?" Eric said laughing.

"Today has been a good day, that's all, and no, my feet don't hurt," Rose said as she continued to smile.

"Oh, I'm so sorry, Eric, this is my friend Coffee."

"Hi you doing, Coffee? I'm Eric."

"I know. We all know. Rose reminds us all the time," she smilingly said.

"Oh, yeah?" Eric said blushing.

"Eric, Eric, Eric, especially today. My baby Eric this, my Eric that."

"That's enough, Coffee, you're home now," Rose said as the car pulled onto her block.

"Twenty-three nineteen, that's my house," Coffee said, pointing to a house in the middle of the block.

Pulling up in front of her house, Coffee thanked Eric for the ride and got out. Once she was safely inside, Eric pulled off.

"I'm hungry, Eric. Can we go get something to eat?"

"Yeah, where do you want to go?"

"Anywhere, it don't matter."

"We can go by Dave & Buster's on Delaware Avenue."

"Okay, that's fine," Rose said as she continued to smile.

Entering Dave & Buster's Restaurant...

A short waitress in a blue and yellow tight outfit escorted Eric and Rose to a table. The restaurant was only half crowded on this weekday night. After ordering their food, Eric and Rose began talking.

"Why are you so happy tonight, Rose?"

"Today has been very special. I talked to my father and everything is looking good."

"What did your pop say?"

"Oh, my dad says so much, but he always gives me good advice."

The waitress then walked up holding two plates of fried shrimp. After eating their food and paying their bill, Eric and Rose left the restaurant. Driving out of the parking lot, Eric flowed into the hectic traffic on Delaware Avenue.

"Girl, you been cheezing all night. What's going on with you?" Eric said.

"Tonight is special. Can't I be happy?" Rose smiled.

"What's so special about tonight?"

Going inside her Guess Jeans jacket pocket, Rose pulled out a set of keys.

"What's that?" Eric said.

"Keys," Rose said smiling.

"Keys to what?" Eric asked.

"Keys to where I want you to make love to me tonight."

"What!" Eric said, driving through a red light.

"Eric, I don't want to go home tonight. I want to stay with you tonight."

"Are you sure, Rose? Where did this come from?"

"I never been more sure in my life. Tonight I want you to make love to me."

"Do you think you're ready?"

"I know I'm ready. I want you to be my first," Rose said with a serious look now on her face.

"Rose, I can wait. You don't have to if you're not really sure."

"Eric, I'm sure and I can't wait any longer," Rose said with her hand now rubbing the back of Eric's neck.

Shaking the keys in her other hand, Rose said, "And this is where I want to go."

Twenty minutes later, Center City Philadelphia, The Marriott Hotel, Suite 421...

"I don't believe you, Rose. How? When?"

"Earlier today at work. I called the hotel and made reservations for two. I couldn't believe it when I asked was suite 421 vacant tonight and was told yes, that it wasn't occupied. I didn't care what it cost. Tonight I knew I had to have you and I wanted it to be special, that's why I left work early."

"I don't believe you went out of your way like this," Eric said, impressed because no woman had ever done anything like this for him before.

"I'm sorry. I couldn't get the limo and rose petals, but here," she said going into the closet and coming back out with a small brown teddy bear.

"Girl, you are full of many surprises, I see."

"Just like you," Rose said smiling and laying the teddy bear on the dresser.

"I still can't believe you got the same room," Eric said looking around.

"Maybe it's fate. Some things are just inevitable," Rose said sitting on the bed.

"Rose, this is a very expensive room."

"If this was about money, we wouldn't be here."

"No girl ever went out of their way like this for me before," Eric said staring into Rose's beautiful dark brown eyes.

"Maybe that's the problem."

"What?"

"I'm not a girl," she said grabbing Eric's hand. "I'm a woman."

Sitting on the bed next to Rose, they began passionately kissing.

Eric then began to slowly take off all Rose's clothes. And all of his as well. Seeing Rose's erect nipples, Eric began kissing around her soft breasts with his tongue. Eric touched places on Rose's body that she never knew existed. Feelings she never knew were inside of her were now being released. Her strong moans turned him on as he continued to taste every dimension of Rose's never explored territory.

Slowly licking Rose around her clit, her nails dug into his flesh, scratching off skin with every lick of his mesmerizing tongue. Her wetness instantly turned the king size bed into a small stream. Never had she experienced a feeling so good as she had multiple orgasms, and didn't even understand what was happening or what was going on with her trembling body. All she knew was the feeling was unbelievable.

As she continued to moan to this wonderful feeling she had never known before, Eric laid on top of her. Slowly spreading Rose's legs apart, Eric gently inserted all of himself into the wetness of Rose's tight paradise. Into this wonderful rainforest where he was the first to ever explore. The first to ever succeed, he began stroking. Never had she felt a pain like this as he filled her with every inch of himself till there was no more. And at the same time, never had she felt a pleasure this intense and so incredible.

The feelings turned her moans into screams as she experienced orgasm over and over again. "I love you, Rose. I love you," Eric said as the sweat rolled down his face.

"I love you, Eric," Rose said with a scream that could be heard through the halls. "Eric, oh, Eric," she said, biting him on his chest. Doing anything she could do to control the next orgasm that was quickly approaching. "I love you, Eric. I love you," she cried out with excitement.

"Ahhhhhhhhh, ohhhhhhhh," Eric yelled out as he finally

came, unloading every drop into her already wet utopia. While at the same time, Rose had an orgasm again, soaking the already wet bed. Both exhausted and tired, Eric laid back and Rose laid on his chest.

"Eric, I love you. I really do," Rose said with tears still rolling down her face.

"I love you too, baby."

"My body feels funny," Rose said as her body was still shaking from the orgasm after effects. "But I can get use to it," Rose said smiling. "I love the way you make me feel, the way you took your time," she said. "It felt so good. I'm glad you are my first."

"I got something to tell you," Eric said.

"What, tell me."

"That's the first time I ever made love to a woman."

"What!" Rose said sitting up.

"No, I mean I've been with girls before. I had sex, but tonight I realized being with you, Rose, was the first time I ever made love in my life. The first time I ever gave all of myself to a woman, emotionally as well as physically, tonight was truly the first time I ever made love to a woman."

"Eric, I think you're my soul mate."

"Your soul mate?" Eric said smiling.

"Yeah, I think we were meant to be together."

"I think so too," Eric said as they both began kissing, then eventually they started making love all over again.

All in the magical room of Suite 421. Tonight the two of them became one and they would both go to a place where neither had known until tonight, to the depth of each other's heart and soul.

Chapter Fifteen

Wednesday morning, the next day...

Driving down City Line Avenue, Eric and Rose pulled into Saks Fifth Avenue's parking lot and got out of the car.

"Eric, you don't have to," Rose said.

"I want you to have the best. If I want to take you shopping and show you off, then that's what I'm going to do," Eric said as he and Rose walked into the store. "Are you going to get in trouble with your job?"

"No, I just called out sick. I had a few sick days and my boss is cool," Rose said smiling.

As Eric and Rose were looking around, a short white woman walked up to them. "Is there anything I can help y'all with?"

"Yes, ma'am, can you please show us the latest in women's fashion that your store has to offer?" Eric said.

"Yes sir, can you please follow me this way," she said walking down the hall and stopping at the Prada section.

"This is a new piece that just came in yesterday," she said, pointing to a white Prada shirt with matching shorts.

"Oh, this is cute," Rose said, taking it off the wall. "How much is it?"

"It's $250. for the set," the lady said.

"Oh, Eric, that is too expensive," Rose said putting it back on the wall.

"Is this the only color it comes in, miss?" Eric asked.

"No, there are four different colors. There's also yellow, blue and red."

"Can you please bring us one of each. What's your size, Rose?"

"No, Eric, that's too much," Rose said.

"What's your size, Rose?"

"I'm a size 4."

"A size 4, miss," Eric said.

The lady quickly walked to the back.

"Eric, that's a thousand dollars," Rose said.

"So? It's just money. Just chill baby. I got this," Eric said, putting his arm around Rose and kissing her on the cheek. "Just chill."

A few moments later, the woman walked back out holding the four outfits in her hand.

"Miss, do you have a cart?" Eric asked looking around.

"Yes, over there," she said pointing to the corner.

"Well, we are going to need one," Eric said.

Walking through every section of the store, anything that Rose wanted, Eric bought for her. After almost an hour of shopping, the cart was full with some of the most recognized names in today's fashion. And the most expensive. Prada short sets, Donna Karan jeans, Gucci shoes and sandals, Chanel purse, Dolce & Gabbana pants, Liz Claiborne dresses, Fendi short sets with matching purse and sneakers. They all had a new friend and her name was Rose.

"Will that be it, sir?" the lady asked smiling at Eric and Rose who couldn't keep their hands off one another.

"Is that it, Rose?" Eric asked approaching the glass counter to pay for everything.

"Yes, baby, that's it. That's enough," Rose said putting her clothes on the counter.

After ringing everything up, the lady looked at the receipt. "Four thousand, fifty-three dollars. Will that be with cash or credit card?" she asked.

"Cash," Eric said, reaching into his baggy Guess jean pockets and pulling out a neat stack of hundred dollar bills with a thick rubber band keeping 'em all in order. "That's $5,000, miss," Eric said handing the money to her behind the counter.

After counting the money and making sure no bill was counterfeit, the lady passed Eric his change and receipt. "Thank you," she said.

"Here you go, miss," Eric said, leaving a hundred dollar bill on top of the glass counter. "Thank you very much," he said as he and Rose grabbed all of their bags and walked out the door.

After shopping, Eric and Rose went and got something to eat. Afterwards, Eric dropped Rose off at home with all of her new gifts.

Wednesday afternoon, at the crib ...

Mike, Braheem and Larry all sat around Eric at the kitchen table. "I talked to the man about the building on 38th and Chestnut Street."

"What did he say?" Mike asked.

"He's going to sell it to us. He's asking for $140,000 cash for the property."

"That's it?" Braheem said.

"Yeah, I told him our lawyer would be contacting him soon,

and that we would love to buy the property as soon as possible. The building is three stories, perfect for a day care," Eric said.

"Soon we will buy more buildings and fix them all up into daycares," Braheem said.

"One at a time," Mike said smiling.

"What do you think, Larry?" Eric asked.

"It's okay, but I think we should buy a club. That's where the money's at. The women!"

"That's where the trouble's at," Eric said. "All you think about is them damn girls. That's why you're always stressing over some chick. I meant to tell you, you look like you been losing a lot of weight. Them girls ain't going nowhere, Larry. Calm down," Eric said laughing. "So everyone who thinks this is a good idea please raise ya hand."

Mike raised his hand, then Braheem and Eric also. As everyone looked at Larry, he finally put his hand in the air.

"I still think we should buy a club," Larry said.

"Okay, it's official. We'll buy the building as soon as everything is taken care of by the realtors and our lawyer," Eric happily said.

Later that evening ...

It's called, *"Never Leave Your Side,"* Rose said to Joyce talking to her on the phone.

"Go head, Rose. Let me hear it," Joyce said.

"Okay, here you go, Joyce."

"You can always count on me, I will always be your strength,
When others leave you stranded, I will go that extra length.
My king, I'm your queen and together we will grow.
Wherever life should take you, I'll follow you and go.

No bars can keep me away, no time will break us apart,
As long as I'm your queen, you'll always have my heart.
I will stand by your side, I will wait till we're both called to God.
If this world that we live in breaks you, I'll be there to help you survive.
I will never run, never break, never surrender,
My love will last from the first of January to the end of December.
Through rain and snow, through winter and fall,
Through spring and summer, you'll have my all.
Till our souls both leave us, and cruise that heavenly ride,
I'll never leave my king; I'll never leave his side."

"Oh, that is beautiful, Rose. That is a beautiful poem," Joyce said.

"I just wanted to write something for all the real sisters who're out there holding it down for their men, their kings."

"What made you write that?"

"Seeing how much my mother loves my father. Even though he's locked up and doing life, that's still the only man she wants in her life."

"That is so real girl, that is so real," Joyce said.

Later that night ...

Outside the Platinum Club, Eric sat in his car waiting for Rose to come out. Inside a small private room, Rose and Mr. Perotta were talking.

"Rose, you sure this is what you want to do?"

"Yes, Mr. Perotta. I'm finished, thank you so much for giving me the job."

"You're my best dancer, beautiful. How could I ever replace

you?"

"Coffee is good and Fire is real good too. You'll be okay."

"Yeah, but they're not like you, Rose. Please stay on for just a few more weeks."

"I'm sorry, Mr. Perotta, but this is it. I promised my boyfriend that I wouldn't do it anymore."

"Okay, okay," he said passing her a stack of money and a white card with his number on it. "It's $1,000, your final pay. If you ever need me for anything, you know you can call," he said. "For anything."

"I know, and thank you for everything, Mr. Perotta."

"That other offer is still on the table, Rose, whenever you want it."

"Mr. Perotta, stop. I already told you a dozen times, all I do is dance, but if I ever need a job, I'll be sure to call you."

"You promise?" he said with a lustful look on his face.

"Yes, I promise," Rose said, grabbing her bag and walking out the door.

Rose noticed Eric when she walked out the side door of the club. Getting inside his car, he pulled off.

"What took you so long?"

"My boss, that old man be tripping."

"Oh, yeah, what's he talking about?"

"He just always trying to pay somebody for sex. He's been liking me ever since I've started."

"What! Old pervert," Eric laughed.

"Yeah, he's an old Italian trick. He done had sex with almost every girl there. He didn't want me to quit, said I was his favorite and all that kinda stuff."

"Well, too bad. What's that?" Eric said pointing at her hand.

"It's my pay and his personal card he gave me. I don't need

this," she said sitting the white card inside the ashtray.

"I have some good news, baby," Eric said.

"What is it?" Rose asked.

"Me and the guys are going to buy a building and turn it into a daycare for less fortunate children. You know, for women in the projects and stuff."

"Oh, that is so nice, Eric."

"Maybe you can help. You know about business. You know how to organize things."

"Oh, I would love to, Eric. When?"

"Next week my lawyer is going to purchase the property. Then we will begin putting together our plans for the daycare center."

"Did you think of a name for it?"

"No, not yet, but I want something that the kids will relate to."

"Eric, that is so nice that you're doing something like this for poor children."

"I was poor once. I know how it is when you don't have nothing and nobody seems to care. When I was young, I loved basketball, but all the courts in the playground were torn down. I had to play on plastic crates. I would always say when I grow up, I'm going to be rich and I'm going to go back to my neighborhood and buy brand new basketball rims for the kids. When I first started hustling, and making money, the first thing I did was buy all new basketball rims for all the courts in the projects. That was one of my happiest days ever in my life."

Pulling up in front of the projects, Eric found an empty space and parked. "All my life, all I wanted to do was make a difference. All I ever knew was the ghetto life and the projects."

"You do make a difference, Eric. You touch so many lives. You are a blessing for so many people," Rose said grabbing

Eric's hand. "You are a king in this urban jungle," Rose said smiling.

"And what are you?"

"Your queen, your queen that will never leave your side."

Eric smiled as they began passionately kissing. Once Eric had walked Rose up to her apartment and made sure she was safe, he got back into his car and drove home.

Chapter Sixteen

Thursday morning ...

Larry, Bunny and another female were all inside of the Blue Moon Motel at 51ˢᵗ Street. A few rolled up joints were laying on the dresser next to a half ounce of powder cocaine and a bottle of Alize. The three of them were all naked, laying on a bed where they had been all night long.

"Come on, baby, let me suck that big black dick. Let me have some now," Bunny said, watching Larry fucking her stripper girlfriend Heaven from the back.

"Okay, okay. Come here. There's enough for you too," Larry said, smiling at Bunny who was feeling left out of the party.

Larry then laid back on the bed as Bunny crawled over to him and began performing a wonderful job of oral sex on him.

While Bunny had every inch of Larry's hard dick in her mouth, Heaven started licking Bunny's pussy, driving her wild and out of control. After Larry came and Bunny swallowed every drop, he laid back and watched as the two women began to make love to each other.

Laying back, snorting a handful of powder cocaine up his nose, Larry enjoyed the x-rated show. As the two women pleased one another over and over again, he just watched. After the two women had finished, Larry pulled out a large stack of money from his jeans pockets. Standing up on top of the bed with a stack of hundred dollar bills in his hand, he yelled out, "Who's the man? Who the motha fucking man?" he shouted loudly once again so everyone could hear.

"You are, Daddy, you are," Bunny said with her arms wrapped around his legs, pumping his ego even more.

Half drunk Larry continued. "That's right. I'm the man, not Scarface, not Nino Brown, not even Eric. I'm the man! I'm the motha fuckin' man!" he said, throwing the money in the air and watching it slowly fall down all over the room.

Later that afternoon, inside the visiting room at Lewisburg Maximum Prison, walking from the inmate's exit, Johnny Ray saw Eric sitting at a table.

"I didn't expect y'all today. Where's Rose, Eric?" Johnny Ray said, walking up, shaking Eric's hand.

"She's not here. I came alone."

"You came by yourself?"

"Yes, Rose is at work. I drove up here to talk to you by myself, sir."

"What's wrong? Is there a problem, Eric?"

"I just wanted to talk to you."

"About what?"

"About Rose."

"What about Rose, Eric?" Johnny Ray said, sitting down in an empty chair.

"Johnny Ray, I want to marry your daughter. I want to make her my wife and spend the rest of my life with her. Out of respect, I wanted to come to you first. It's very important to me to have your blessing. Johnny Ray, I love your daughter more than life itself. For her I would die a thousand times for her happiness and a thousand more just to see her smile."

"Eric, as a man, I have a lot of respect for you and I believe you truly love my daughter. You're a rare man indeed. Just to have come up here to ask me for my daughter's hand in marriage. Truly a man of a different breed. In a class that many will never reach. But as much as it hurts me to say this, my answer is no, Eric."

Eric sat silently as Johnny Ray continued on.

"I believe everything you said is true. In your eyes I could see cupid appear every time at the mention of my Rose's name. But your lifestyle is what I fear when it comes to my only daughter. The life you live and game you play is unhealthy for any woman. And I would never again as a man, a father, take or let my family go through the agony of what our lifestyle does to those who we love. It's always bringing pain to those that are close to us. What I did to my wife, my children, I must live with until my last days. And I am the only one to blame. Yes, I think you are a good man with a good heart. But for me to give you my blessing to take my daughter's hand in marriage would be the second biggest mistake I ever made in my life. The first being me coming here to prison.

"Like I said, as a man I have respect for you. Not too many men would have driven up here to confront a man faced with spending the rest of his life in prison to ask for his daughter's hand. I truly admire that. But the answer will remain no. In order for you, Eric, to have my blessing, you must walk away from the game.

"I know how hard it is to walk away from something you created, something you built, but if you want me to release to you my first child, my only daughter, my Rose, my queen, you must give up the game and walk away or you will never have my blessings. I'm sorry."

Eric sat with his head down as Johnny Ray stood up and just

walked away leaving Eric sitting all alone, even more confused than he ever had been in his life. But at the same time, understanding where Johnny Ray was coming from as a father of a child.

North Philadelphia, a few hours later...

"I got your page, Jose, so I just came straight here," Eric said shaking his Dominican friend's hand. "What's up? Why didn't you just call me?"

"I needed to talk to you in person, Eric."

"Jose, what's wrong?"

"I have a serious problem that I need taken care of immediately."

"What? Where?"

"His name is Felipe Vargas and he's in Miami."

"Miami!" Eric said, scratching the top of his head.

"Eric, my friend, this is very important. Just like your situation was with you when you asked me for my help and I sent Jose, Nino and Raul to handle your business for you. Today I ask the same in return. If I send any of them, they would immediately be recognized by one of Felipe's men and death will be certain. That is why I need you and someone who you really trust with your own life to kill Felipe Vargas for me."

"But ..."

"It's a long story, Eric, but I will give you the short version. Eighteen years ago on our small island, me and Felipe were once best friends. Together we sold thousands of kilos of cocaine to many of our American customers. But Felipe's greed had begun to get the best of him as he eventually cut all ties with me, wanting all the money to himself. In an undercover drug sting by the U.S. Coast Guards, Felipe and his crew were captured transporting 5,000 kilos from the Dominican Republic to Florida. This was two years after me and Felipe had been partners. After pressure from U.S. special prosecutors, Felipe became an informant for the United States government. After Felipe had turned in all of his suppliers, he then turned against me. Me and my entire family. My father, bless is soul, died four years after Felipe turned him in, getting him a 20-year sentence, where he died in a U.S. prison in Atlanta.

"My brother is still serving his 15-year sentence, along with my sister."

"Your sister," Eric said.

"Yes, Felipe's wife. He was married to my sister and she too he turned in to prevent himself from coming to serve time in a U.S. prison. As for me, I was sentenced to seven years and eight months, the least of all my family members.

"When I was released from prison, I was deported back to my country where I had searched to find Felipe for what he had done to me and my loved ones, and kill him with my bare hands. When I was told that he was now living in the U.S., I quickly had illegal passports and my papers forged to come to the United States and track Felipe down. For years, I have been unsuccessful, until a few days ago.

"I received a phone call from a close and dear friend named Juan, who had seen Felipe and immediately called me back here in Philadelphia. He had information to where Felipe was staying and where he would eat dinner at every night with his two body-guards. The place where he eats his meals is called Pierre's Night Club.

"But, what Felipe don't know is Juan, who is my close friend, is also the owner of Pierre's Night Club."

"When do you want me to go to Miami, Jose?"

"Tonight."

"Tonight! Catch a plane tonight?" Eric shockingly said.

"Yes, my young friend, and these are your instructions," Jose said passing Eric a small white piece of paper.

"Tonight I need you to catch a plane to Miami, where someone will meet you and your friend at the airport, and everything will be explained to you for what you have to do. Have you ever been to Miami?"

"Yes, I've been there a lot. I know the city pretty well," Eric said.

"Tomorrow night, there is a very important party that will be taking place at Pierre's Night Club, and you must be there. Tomorrow might be my last opportunity to ever get my revenge for what Felipe has done to me and my family. And my dear father."

"Okay, Jose, I'll leave tonight."

"Thank you, Eric, I will know once you arrive in Miami, but most important, I look forward to your safe return back to Philadelphia, my friend."

Eric then shook Jose's hand and walked out the door.

Driving in his car, Eric called Rose on his cell phone.

"Hello," she said answering.

"Hey, baby."

"Hey, Eric, I been thinking about you all day, baby. Are you coming by?"

"No, I have to go somewhere tonight."

"Where?"

"I got to go to Miami."

"Miami, why? What's in Miami?"

"Rose, it's an emergency. It's nothing. I just got to go take care of some business. I'll be back Saturday."

"Eric, is everything okay?"

"Baby, stop worrying. Everything is fine. I'll call you tonight from my hotel room."

"You promise me?"

"I promise baby. I'll be back sooner than you think."

"I love you, Eric, please be safe," Rose said in a sad voice.

"I love you, Rose. I promise everything will be all right. Bye," Eric said closing up his cell phone and pulling into his apartment complex parking lot. After getting himself together, Eric and Braheem headed to the airport.

Miami International Airport, a few hours later ...

"The instructions say to wait by this phone booth," Eric said to Braheem.

"Well, we been here for 20 minutes already. When is this limo gonna get here?"

"It will be here. Just calm down."

A long black Lincoln limousine suddenly turned the corner. Driving up to the phone booth, a window was rolled down.

"Are you Eric?" a man said pointing to Braheem.

"No, he's Eric," Braheem said pointing to Eric.

"Oh, I'm sorry. I'm Juan. I'm Jose's friend. Please, hurry and get in."

Opening the door, Eric and Braheem both got into the limo.

"Are y'all hungry?"

"No," both men said at the same time.

"Do you have the instructions?"

"Yes. Here they go," Eric said, passing Juan the white piece of paper.

"Thank you. Here, this is the new instructions," he said, passing them another piece of paper. "Everything you need to know is on there. When the job is done, burn it as soon as possible."

Pulling up in front of a Holiday Inn hotel, the limo stopped.

"Here are your keys," Juan said. "Everything is paid for. There is $5,000 in cash inside the bottom dresser drawer if you two want to enjoy yourself tonight."

Eric took the keys and he and Braheem got out of the limo.

"I will see you both tomorrow. Good luck."

Once Eric and Braheem were inside the hotel lobby, the limo pulled off and drove up the street.

Later that night, Eric was laying in bed talking on the telephone. "I told you that I would call you."

"I was just worried, Eric."

"I told you, Rose, you don't have to worry, that I'll be okay."

"I miss you already."

"I miss you too, baby," Eric said.

"My father called today."

"Oh, yeah, what did he tell you?"

"He said that you came by to visit him."

"That's it?"

"Yeah, that was all. He said that he really enjoyed your visit. Something about hopefully you'll make the right decision. What's that all about?" Rose asked.

"Nothing. We was just having a man-to-man talk."

"My father likes you I see."

"Did he say that?"

"Yeah, he said that you are in a class by yourself. I told him I know." Rose smilingly said.

"Baby, I'm tired," Eric said yawning. "Can I call you tomorrow. I'm very sleepy."

"Okay, baby, I'll let you catch some z's," Rose said.

"I love you, Rose."

"I love you, Eric. Goodnight," she said hanging up the phone.

After hanging up the telephone, Eric turned off his bed-room light and went to sleep.

Chapter Seventeen

Friday afternoon ...

Mike and Larry were inside the crib talking.

"I told you, Larry, for the last time, the answer is no. Tonight is the last time that I'll serve Mario and Vinny."

"But what about all the money we can be making, Mike?"

"I don't care about all the money. You can keep it all. I'm going to focus on the daycares. Eric said in a year we would have about three or four up and running all around the city, in poor neighborhoods."

"Eric, Eric, Eric, that's all you think about. That's just why he ain't take neither of us to Miami. He ain't even ask. All we get is a lousy phone call telling us he's in Miami and he'll be back in a few days."

"So what? He's taking care of some important business."

"I bet he's down there with some fine Cuban model having the time of his life, him and Braheem, or they might even be making some moves without us, without cutting us in."

"Eric wouldn't do that and you know it."

"I don't know nothing. All I know is I'm still in fucked up southwest Philly and him and Braheem are in sunny, hot, beautiful Miami, Florida. You better wake up, Mike. Your best friend ain't all what you think."

"How could you say that after all he's done for you?"

"What, a lousy car, an apartment, a few dollars here and there. I could have gotten all that by my damn self. If I was getting what he is getting from the Dominicans, I would be the man too."

"You better not ever let Eric hear you talk like this."

"You think I'm afraid of Eric? Once I make this sale, I was going to start buying my own weight and go solo anyway. I'm tired of being some petty ass middleman. Mike, you can stay under another man's balls. I'm a get mine and step off."

"That would be stupid, Larry."

"No, that would be smart. Eric pays us 25, 35 thousand a month. When I can make double that in 10 minutes, I ain't nobody's fool."

"But we all one family, and he said we would all be millionaires in a few years if we stick to the plan."

"No, y'all are all one big family. You're his best friend and Braheem is his cousin. I'm just a guy he met in high school who use to take up for him. Now look at him. He thinks he's the motha fuckin' man."

"I don't believe that's how you feel about Eric. We got something good right here and you gonna fuck it all up."

"No, I'm not, because after tonight, I'm going to be doing my own thing and you should help me, if you're smart. We can both be like Eric, both be filthy rich."

"No, I told you, Larry. Tonight is my last time. You can say what you want and do what you're going to do, quit or whatever, but I'm all right. I'll never shit on my man. I'll never forget all that Eric's done for me. He's like my brother, like I thought the two of y'all was," Mike said in a sad voice.

"We are, Kane and Able," Larry angrily said. "Kane and mother fuckin' Able."

Thirtieth Street, U.S. Post Office ...

"Eric will be okay," Joyce said trying to cheer her friend up.

"I hope so, Joyce. I'm just scared."

"He can take care of himself. He's been on these streets a long time, he ain't make it all this way for nothing."

"I didn't want to really sweat him about his business, but I hope he didn't go to Miami to see no other girl."

"Rose, Eric loves you to death. I ain't never seen him trip over no female like he does you. Nobody! That boy ain't never call me before and ask me about some chick, plus he has always been a loyal man. Eric has respect for you and for himself."

Rose smiled as the tears rolled down from her eyes. "I just don't understand why he just got up and went to Miami. Just like that, something just ain't right. He could tell me what's going on. I would do anything for him, anything he asks me, I would do," Rose said.

"And he would do the same for you. That boy is crazy in love with you. He's probably thinking about you right now. Missing his precious Rose," Joyce said.

Wiping her tears with her shirt, "Yeah, you're probably right, Joyce. I don't know why I'm tripping. I just can't keep going through this. This love stuff is driving me crazy. I knew I should have stayed single," Rose said as she and Joyce started laughing together, as they both finished separating the piles of mail that was in front of them.

Friday night ...

The sky was very dark on this chilly Friday night, as Mike and Larry pulled into the garage lot on 6th Street in south Philadelphia. Getting out of Mike's cherry red Lexus, he and Larry both cautiously looked around for anything suspicious or anything that seemed different.

"Everything is all right," Larry said, taking the large trash bag from the trunk of his car.

"I'm just making sure," Mike said, touching his hip to make sure his 45 caliber handgun was safely tucked on his side.

Closing the trunk, Larry walked over to Mike.

"Do you have your vest on, Larry?"

"Yeah, always, but we ain't got to worry about that. Mario and Vinny are cool. Stop tripping."

Walking to the back door, Larry tapped on it three times then waited. After seeing who it was, Mario opened the door.

"Hey, what's up fellas?" he said inviting them both inside.

Vinny then walked into the room, holding a large brown briefcase.

"What's been going on, fellas. Let's make this quick," he said putting the briefcase on a table.

Opening the briefcase up, the neatly stacked large bills were all packed inside. "It's all there, $500,000 cash. Just like before," Mario said, passing the briefcase to Larry.

"Count it and see," Vinny said.

"I trust you, Mario," Larry said, closing the briefcase. "Here, this is y'alls," he said, passing the large bag of kilos of cocaine to Mario. "Twenty-five keez," Larry said.

Mario dumped the bag and cut open one of the bricks of coke. Tasting it with his finger, he shook his head to Vinny, letting him know that it was the proper stuff. Both Vinny and Mario began putting each brick back into the large trash bag.

Suddenly, pulling out a 357 magnum from under his jacket, Vinny had the powerful handgun pointed at Larry's forehead.

"What's going on?" Larry said in a now scared voice.

"Shut the fuck up!" Mario said as he pulled out a black 9 mm with an infrared beam and silencer attached to it.

"Don't try it," Mario said to Mike who seemed to be easing his hand toward his hip.

"Try it, and you'll be a dead ass nigger," Mario said slowly walking over to Mike, taking his gun from off his hip.

"Mario. Vinny. I thought we was partners," Larry begged.

"I said shut the fuck up, mooley," Mario said in an angry voice.

"I fuckin' told you something wasn't right," Mike said, looking at Larry.

"Yeah, you should have listened, then tonight wouldn't be y'all last," Vinny said, pointing his gun.

Reaching into his jacket pocket, Mario pulled out a small walkie talkie radio. Turning it on, he spoke into it.

"We're ready," he said. "Everything is perfect," then he cut it off and put it back into his jacket pocket.

Vinny walked up and grabbed the briefcase that was now laying on the floor. Opening it up, he took all the real hundred dollar bills from off top of all the cut up newspaper stacks that were underneath.

"And this idiot didn't even count his fuckin' money," Vinny said laughing.

Outside, a black 1979 Cadillac Fleetwood pulled up to the door and beeped its loud horn.

"Okay, fellas, we're all going for a ride," Mario said, pointing his 9 mm at Mike's head.

Opening the side door, Vinny grabbed the bag of kilos and walked outside first. A short white guy with a long black ponytail was sitting behind the wheel.

"Hurry up, fellas," he said, popping open the large Cadillac trunk.

"Come on, let's go," Mario said as Mike and Larry both walked out the back door.

Lifting up the trunk, Mario told them both to get in, as Vinny was walking back around from putting the bag of cocaine in the back seat of the car. Soon as Vinny walked up, Larry swung, hitting him the face and knocking the gun from his hand, and immediately started running. Mike thought about it, but before he could raise his fist, two quiet 9 mm bullets were already inside of his brains. As his body slumped to the ground, Mario immediately ran after Larry.

"Get that motha fucker," the driver said getting out of the car.

Finally finding his gun on the ground, Vinny followed after Mario. Running around the front of the garage, Larry was long gone, nowhere in sight. Mario and Vinny finally walked back to the car.

Mike's fading life still appeared to be alive, shaking on the ground. Mario stood over him and shot him two more times in the head, this time making sure the last two bullets had done their job the first two didn't.

Picking up Mike's dead corpse and throwing it in the trunk, Mario told the short man to "Hurry up and get rid of it."

As he closed the trunk and they all got inside of the car, they quickly drove away.

Only 21 years old, Mike was now dead, tragically becoming a victim of the one thing that he feared most ... **the cruel game.**

Forty-five minutes later ...

Larry walked into the crib, scared. Sweating and nervously shaking, he sat down on the couch. Picking up the telephone, he called Bunny on her cell phone.

"The number is no longer in service," the voice recording

said.

"Bitch!" Larry said, scratching his head, confused with his current state of mind. "That bitch!" he said, slamming the phone down. "They fucking killed Mike," he said as he began to tear up. "They set us up, them motha fuckin' snakes. Oh, my God! Mike is dead."

Pulling out a small pack of powder cocaine, Larry inhaled every grain up his nose. "They killed Mike. They set us up. And they got the drugs. Them fuckin' snakes," he continued to say as he balled his fist together in anger.

"What the fuck am I going to do? Eric will kill me if he found out I was involved. That bitch. I'm going to kill that bitch, Bunny. I don't believe this shit. Mike is dead," he said now pacing around the room. "What the fuck can I do? They set me the fuck up, them fucking two snakes," Larry said talking to himself.

"Mike! Oh, Mike. I'm sorry," he yelled out in the empty apartment. "God, please forgive me," he screamed out and began crying.

Laying on the floor, all Larry could do tonight was hope this was all a bad dream or a nightmare he was having. But in the morning, he would wake up to find out that it was all real, and Mike would no longer be coming back.

Chapter Eighteen

Eleven o'clock that same night ...

At South Beach Miami, Pierre's Night Club, the temperature was in the high 70s on this beautiful Miami night. Outside this popular club, some of the most expensive cars in the world were showcased. A grey Aston Martin, a silver Rolls Royce. A red Ferrari was parked next to a yellow Lamborgini Diablo. Tonight, Peirre's Night Club was the place to be and everybody who was anybody was there.

Inside the large lavish club, the dance floor was packed with partygoers. A million lights all seemed to be blinking at the same time. The club was filled with some of the most beautiful women in Miami. The private booths laid against the walls, each with their own two waiters assigned to answer any beckon call of the rich and famous.

Everyone seemed to be inside, from politicians to entertainers. Movie stars to rap stars, Wall Street dealers to drug dealers. The real ballers and players!

The house music was loudly playing as Felipe and his two large bodyguards sat inside a private booth drinking champagne and talking business.

"Is everything okay, Mr. Felipe?" Juan said, walking up to his private booth.

"Everything is fine, Juan. Why don't you join us?" Felipe said pouring his champagne into his glass.

"I wish I could, but it's so busy tonight. I'm sorry," Juan said.

"The women in here are so beautiful and the music is very good," Felipe said.

"I'm so glad that you are enjoying yourself, Mr. Felipe. If there's anything you need, anything at all, please be kind and use the two young workers I have specially for you." Juan said as he pointed to both waiters.

"Thank you very much, Juan. I surely appreciate this," Filipe said.

"Have a good night, Mr. Filipe," Juan said walking away and disappearing into the crowd.

"Do y'all have lobster?" Felipe asked the two waiters.

"Yes," the tall blond haired, blue eyed man said with his movie star looks.

"Can you please bring me the largest you have?"

"Yes, sir, will that be all?" the short gay waiter with dark curly hair said holding a pad and pen in his hand.

"You can bring me another bottle of this champagne too."

"Okay, sir, we will be right back," the waiter said as he and his partner both walked through the crowd together.

"I love this place. This is the best club in Miami. In Florida!" Mr. Felipe said, drinking his last bit of champagne and laughing out loud.

A few moments later...

As Mr. Felipe and his two bodyguards sat enjoying the loud music, the dancing crowd paid no attention to the two men both dressed in waiter outfits holding small shiny trays in their hands with their faces fully covered in dark black makeup.

Walking through the crowded club, the two men quickly approached Mr. Felipe's booth. Before he could react and his body guards could reach for the guns that they both were carrying, the two masked men had already pulled out two loaded 9 mm with attached silencers from under their trays. Without hesitation, they began firing every single bullet into the head and body of Felipe and his two large bodyguards, instantly killing the three of them. They quickly walked through the dancing crowd of partygoers who had no idea what had just happened. After walking through the crowd, the two men quickly ran through an open side door. Outside, a Honda CBR900 and a Kawasaki ZX9 were both waiting for them. With the keys already inside the ignition, the two men quickly jumped on the motorcycles and drove away disappearing into the dark Miami night.

When a waiter found the three men all dead inside their private booth, the club was quickly evacuated and the local authorities were called to the club. Once the police arrived and saw the brutal slaying, they began asking questions of the staff and some of the people in the stunned crowd. But no one had seen or heard anything, leaving the police with no clues and no suspects.

Saturday afternoon at the crib in southwest Philly...

Eric's cell phone was ringing as it laid on top of the T.V. waking Larry up from his sleep. He reached up and grabbed it off the T.V. "Hello," Larry said.

"Larry, it's me, Joyce. Is Eric there?" she said crying.

"No, calm down. What's wrong?"

"Mike is dead. It's on the front page of the *Daily News* and all over the T.V."

"What!"

"Everybody in the projects talking about it. It's everywhere."

"Eric ain't back yet. He's supposed to get back today. Him and Braheem went to Miami."

"You didn't know?"

"No, I was asleep all night."

"I been calling all morning long. I don't believe Mike was killed like that."

"What did they say happened?"

"The paper said his body was found floating in the Schuylkill River by two old men. He was shot four times in the head and they also found his Lexus."

"Where?"

"In south Philly on 25th and Grays Ferry Avenue. It was all stripped and sitting on crates. The cops said somebody put it there and think that Mike was kidnapped," Joyce said as she couldn't stop crying.

"Eric is going to go off when he finds out his best friend was killed."

"Do you know what time Eric will be back in Philly?"

"This afternoon, that's all he said."

"I know it's going to be some shit when Eric gets back. He and Mike are like brothers. Them two have been like that ever since they both lived in the projects, ever since they were both kids."

"I know you probably got things to do Larry. I'm so sorry about your friend, my friend. Everybody loved Mike. I'll call back later," Joyce said crying and hanging up the phone.

Hanging up the phone, Larry put on his Air Nike sneakers and walked out the door.

In a private room inside the Platinum Club ...

"You got to find that guy and kill 'em," Mr. Perrotta said.

"We will, Uncle P. Bunny knows how to get in touch with him," Mario said.

"Bunny, do you know where he lives?" asked Vinny.

"He never took me to his house, only to motels. I just got his cell phone number."

"I want that nigger dead," Mr. Perotta said, slamming his fist hard on the table.

"Does he know anything about the club?"

"No, everything was done at the garage," Vinny said.

"He must know now that Bunny was in on it," Mr. Perotta said.

"Uncle P. don't worry yourself. We will find and kill the fuckin' mooley, me and Vinny will make sure this fuckin' guy gets what his friend got. Don't worry, we'll take care of it," Mario confidently said.

"It's all over the damn news. Did you two clean your tracks?"

"The cops will never know who did it. Everything is taken care of," Vinny said.

"This guy Larry knows and who knows what he might do," Mr. Perotta said.

"This guy is a fuckin' crook, a drug dealer, the last thing he wants is some fuckin' cops questioning him," Mario said.

"He's gonna call me, I know he will," Bunny said.

"I thought you stopped your service," Mario asked.

"I did, yesterday, but I will get it turned back on. My friends down at Sprint won't mind turning it back on for me," Bunny said smiling.

"You get it turned on as soon as possible, and you two go

finish looking for that mother fucker and don't come back until you find him," Mr. Perotta said. "Now leave," he said as all three of them walked out the door.

A few moments later, the dancer Heaven knocked on the door and walked in. "Hi, Mr. Perotta," she said smiling, as he sat back in his large black recliner chair.

"Hi, beautiful."

"I wore the angel outfit you like Rose in, just like you asked me to," she said walking up to him and getting on her knees.

"And you look beautiful, just as good as Rose," he said rubbing his hand through her long hair. "Just as good as Rose."

Unzipping his pants, Mr. Perotta pulled out his dick.

"How do you want it, sir?" Heaven politely asked.

"I want your mouth all over it," he said, really wishing she could be Rose.

Heaven then opened her mouth and started sucking every inch of Mr. Perotta, just the way he liked it, but still he wished it was Rose instead.

Philadelphia International Airport ...

Inside a white limo, Eric, Braheem and Jose were all talking.

"Thank you, Eric, very much," Jose said smiling.

"You're welcome, Jose."

"You have eased many years of suffering and many years of pain."

"I'm glad that I could help, Jose."

"If there's anything you ever need, anything at all, you let me know," Jose said.

"I'm fine, Jose, you have done so much for me already."

"Eric, I can't thank you enough. For you, I will always be

there for."

"You did me a favor and I did you one in return. You owe me nothing."

"Eric, you are a man like no other. Someone I truly consider a good friend."

"Thank you, Jose, thank you very much," Eric said as the limo suddenly stopped.

"Okay, Jose, this is where we get out. I will call you soon and I will see you next week."

"Hold up, Eric, before you leave."

"Yes, Jose?"

"You keep that. You owe me not one penny. It's all yours — a gift from me."

"Thank you, Jose. Thank you," Eric said as he and Braheem got out of the limo and shut the door.

As Jose waved goodbye, the limo quickly drove off.

Walking past both their parked cars, Eric and Braheem went inside the crib.

Grabbing his cell phone from off the T.V., Eric immediately called Rose.

"Hello," Rose said, quickly picking up the phone.

"Hey, baby. I'm home," Eric said smiling.

"Eric! Eric! I'm so sorry baby! I'm so sorry!"

"Sorry about what?"

"Oh, you didn't hear yet."

"Hear what? Rose, what are you talking about?"

"I'm sorry to have to be the one who tells you this, Eric, but your friend, Mike, was killed last night. Someone shot him."

"What! Rose who told you this?"

"Eric, I'm so sorry."

"Who told you this, I said."

"It's on the front page and all on T.V.," Rose said crying.

"Are you sure it's Mike?"

"Eric, the whole project was talking about it. Joyce has been calling you all morning."

"No, no. This can't be true. No. Please don't let this be true," Eric screamed.

"What?" Braheem said.

"Rose, I'll call you back. I got to go. I got to find out what happened."

"Eric, please don't do anything crazy. I love you, Eric," she said.

"I love you, Rose. I'll talk to you later," Eric said, shutting up his phone.

"Mike is dead, Braheem. Somebody shot him."

"No, not Mike. Tell me you're joking." Braheem said as tears began rolling down his face.

"It's true. He's dead. We got to find out what's going on. Where the fuck is Larry. He should have been here," Eric said.

"Why ain't he here?"

Eric quickly dialed Larry's cell phone number.

"Hello," Larry said nervously answering his cell phone.

"Where the hell are you, man?"

"I'm home."

"You heard about Mike?"

"No, what's wrong?"

"He's dead!"

"He's dead? What?" Larry shouted. "What happened?"

"Yeah, somebody shot him."

"Come over here right now, Larry, and hurry up." Eric said angrily shutting up his phone.

"No, I don't believe this. Why, God, Why Mike. Why not me?" Eric cried out.

The cell phone started ringing and Eric quickly picked it

up.

"Hello," he said.

"Eric. Eric, it's me, Joyce. Are you okay?"

"Joyce, lil sis, is it true?"

"Yes, Eric, Mike is dead," she said crying into the phone. "I'm so sorry, Eric, I am so sorry."

"Do you know what happened?"

"He was shot and his car was found in south Philly this morning. I called and told Larry. Is he there?"

"No, he's not here."

"He was this morning when I called your cell phone."

"Larry was here?"

"Yeah, I called and told him that Mike was killed. He knows. I'm sorry about Mike, Eric. If you need me for any-thing, call me. It don't matter what time. I left my cell phone number on your phone. Call me if you need me. I love you, Eric. Be strong."

"Bye, lil sis, I'll talk to you later," Eric said as he hung up the phone.

"Why, why, why Mike. Why ...," Eric cried. "God, tell me why," he yelled falling to his knees.

Chapter Nineteen

An hour later ...

Larry walked through the door while Braheem and Eric were sitting on the couch. "What took you so long, Larry?"

I had to take a shower and get dressed. What happened?"

"Mike was killed. That's what happened," Braheem yelled out in anger.

"Where were you last night, Larry?" Eric asked.

"I was home. I went to bed early."

"On Friday night? You?" Braheem said.

"I was tired."

"Larry, stop fuckin' lying. Where the fuck were you last night?" Eric said.

"Eric, I was home. I swear."

"I thought you said you didn't know that Mike was killed."

"I didn't."

"Joyce said she told you this morning when she called here. That you answered my cell phone. Why the fuck are you lying, Larry? You better tell me where the fuck you were," Eric said.

"Eric, I'm sorry. I'm sorry, Eric. Me and Mike were down south Philly."

"Where? What are you talking about, south Philly for what?"

"We went to handle some business."

"What business were y'all handling down south Philly?"

"The guys I told you about, the Italians." Larry said.

"The bitch's brother?"

"Yeah, them. I'm sorry, Eric. I'm sorry. We didn't know. They set us up."

"I fucking told you not to fuck with them guys. I fucking told you. Larry."

"I'm sorry, Eric. I'm sorry," Larry cried.

"What the fuck happened? Tell me what happened."

"A few weeks ago I met with Mario and Vinny and I sold them 5 keez. After that they wanted more. 25, so I needed some more coke. I didn't have enough."

"So you asked Mike?" Eric said.

"Yeah, and Mike agreed to sell his too."

"That's why Mike was acting funny." Eric said. "He wanted to tell me something."

"We sold them 25 keez and they paid us for everyone of 'em."

"Then what?" Braheem said.

"They wanted 25 more keez and we agreed to meet them last night at the garage on 6th Street down south Philly. When we got there, everything seemed normal, but once we were ready to leave, they both pulled out guns, catching us both off guard."

"Then what?" Eric said.

"As we were walking out the door, I kicked Mario and punched Vinny knocking the gun from his hand."

"Then what?" Braheem asked.

"Then me and Mike had both ran. At first he was behind me, then when I looked back, I didn't see him. So I kept running. I ran to a gas station on 9th Street and caught a cab. Then

I told him to drive me back around 6th Street to the garage. When I didn't see Mike or his car, I figured he got away. So I told the cab driver to bring me here. I waited for Mike all night long, but he never showed up."

"Why did you lie then?"

"I was scared. I was confused."

"Why did you do what I told you not to do? Why did you go behind my back?"

"I'm sorry, Eric. I'm very sorry."

"Sorry can't bring Mike back," Eric said. "He's dead because of you."

"I'm sorry I didn't listen. I'm sorry," Larry cried. "That bitch set me up!"

"Who?" Braheem asked.

"Bunny, that bitch from the Platinum Club," Larry said.

"The stripper? The white girl?" Eric said.

"Yeah, she kept telling me about her brother begging me to meet him. That's her uncle's spot. One night when we were in a hotel room she was half drunk and told me she danced for her uncle who owns the club."

"Are you a fucking idiot, Larry. That bitch and her family set you the fuck up. You must have told her your business too and she told her brother and uncle about you. That's what made them set you up. That's why Mike is dead."

"I didn't know. I'm sorry."

"They set y'all up for 25 keez, then were going to kill both of y'all, and no one would have ever known anything. That bitch played you," Eric said.

"That's why she walked up to you in the club that night. She peeped your sweet ass from a mile away. You was nothing but her vick."

Larry sat down shaking his head in disbelief.

"You fell into that bitch's trap. Her brother and her uncle probably spotted you in the club, trickin' and acting a fool, and sent her after you. And your dumb ass fell for it, thinking it was all about your dick. You stupid motha fucka. Ain't no dick in the world stronger than a woman's pussy. Pussy runs the world. The only thing that's stronger than a woman's pussy is a man's mind. Something that most men never use," Eric said staring at Larry with an angry look on his face.

"What are we going to do, Eric?" Larry said.

"We are going to set them up like they did you and Mike."

"How?" Braheem asked.

"We are going to get that bitch, that's how," Eric said. "Somebody is going to pay for what happened to Mike. I swear on my unborn kids, somebody is going to pay for what happened to Mike."

"How are you going to set the girl up?" Braheem asked.

"That bitch is a gold digger. Just like pussy is a man's downfall, money is a ho's downfall. Me and Braheem will go to the club. That bitch will break her neck to fuck us both for the right price. That's how. That's how we will set her up. With money."

"When? When will we do it?" Larry asked.

"Next week. First we got a lot of shit to do. Everything must be done right."

"What do you want me to do, Eric?" Larry asked.

"Nothing. Nothing at all. I will let you know next week, but for now, I don't want you to do shit but chill in the house. Can you do that?"

"Yeah, Eric. I can do that. That won't be a problem," Larry said.

"Braheem will drop you off home and I will call you to keep you up to date on what's going on."

"Why is Braheem going to drop me off? I got my own car."

"No, your old car. That car is going to pay for Mike's funeral. I'm going to sell it and give the money to his family."

"But Eric ..."

"But what? What motha fucka? My best friend is dead. What?"

"Never mind. I think it's a good idea, that's all." Larry said.

"Braheem, take him home. I'll call you later, Larry," Eric said as he walked away into another room.

"Come on, man, come on, let's go," Braheem said opening the front door.

After they both left, Eric walked back into the room and sat down on the couch. As the tears started falling from his eyes, he laid back and tried to cry away his pain. The pain of this cruel game. The pain of revenge ... the pain of how he now looked at Larry. And the pain of losing Mike, his best friend.

Joyce's Ford Taurus was parked outside, in front of the projects. Rose and Joyce were both inside talking about the tragic news of Mike's death. "He was so cool. Everybody loved Mike." Joyce said, showing Rose a picture of her, Eric and Mike when they were all kids playing in the projects. "When we were young, Eric was good at picking locks. He would always pick the lock on the candy machine and give all the candy to me and Mike, and some of the other project's kids. I use to be a little tomboy and Eric and Mike would let me hang out with them. I was the only girl in their gang. We would run through the halls, ringing people's doorbells. We would play on the elevators. They made sure nothing ever happened to me. I was like both their little sister. One time a boy pushed me off my bike and Eric and Mike both beat him up. I still can't believe that Mike is gone. I still can't believe it."

"I got to see Eric. I got to be there for him. I can't let him go through this all alone," Rose said.

"Eric is confused right now. I can't imagine how he feels. He's hurting," Joyce said.

"That's why I need to be there with him, to let him know he's not in this alone and there are people like us who love him," Rose said.

"Did you call him, Rose?"

"Yeah and I could tell he was hurting, but what he don't understand now is that his pain is my pain."

"Eric can be real stubborn at times. He likes to do things at his own pace," Joyce said. "He's always been that way. He's not use to people being there for him. He was always the one there for everybody else. And now the one person who truly cared for him is dead," Joyce said unable to control her falling tears.

"Well he has me now, and I will be there for him, if he likes it or not. I won't let him run away from me," Rose said.

"He has both of us. He knows I would do anything for him. He knows how much Mike meant to me too. Come on, Rose, we are going for a ride," Joyce said.

"Where are we going?" Rose asked.

"Where you need to be," Joyce said, starting up her car.

Joyce drove off with Rose wondering where she was taking her.

On his way home, after dropping Larry off, Braheem drove by a newsstand and bought a paper to read about the loss of his close friend.

The front page of the *Philadelphia Daily News* read: **Man found dead in Schuylkill River**, with a picture of Mike's face on the cover. With his car parked on the side of the road,

Braheem turned to the page to read about the tragic ending of Mike's short life.

"This morning around 5:30 a.m.. two men fishing in the Schuylkill River discovered the naked body of Michael Flemming. Flemming, 21, of southwest Philadelphia. appeared to have been shot at close range numerous times. Police later discovered a 1997 red Lexus that was registered in Flemming's name, stripped, and on crates, off Grays Ferry Avenue in south Philadelphia.

"Homicide detectives said they have very little clues to go on, but believe that the hit appeared to be a mob style execution.

"Any information on this case, or the McDonald's triple homicide case, please contact the Philadelphia Homicide Unit or call your local police station."

Braheem tearfully closed the paper and threw it out the window. "Don't worry about it, Mike, they're gonna pay for what they done to you. All of them. I won't let you down buddy. They're all gonna pay. I promise you," Braheem said as he began driving home.

After leaving Mike's mother's house, where Eric had just dropped off $237,000 dollars, a $37,000 check for selling Larry's Mercedes and the $200,000 that Eric gave out of his own pocket, Eric walked into his apartment and sadly sat on the couch. With his head down, all he could think about was Mike and how life would now be without his best friend around. Laying down on the couch, he closed his eyes.

Hearing a noise from the back room, he quickly sat up and called out to Braheem. "Braheem, is that you?" he said.

No one answered.

Thinking he was just hearing things, he laid back down

closing his eyes once again. Hearing the strange noise again, he jumped up and quickly grabbed his chrome 380 that was on his hip.

"Braheem, are you in there?" he said, standing up with his hand now firmly gripped around the handle of the gun.

With the gun cocked and ready, he slowly walked down the hall. As he walked up to his bedroom door, he noticed it half open. Something he never did. Eric always kept his door shut so he knew someone was there. Slowly kicking the door with his feet, he walked into his room, getting the surprise of his life ...

"Don't shoot. I'm unarmed and undressed," Rose said smiling at the confused and stunned looking Eric.

"Rose, what are you doing here? How did you get in?"

"Joyce let me in," Rose said laying on top of the covers with nothing on her but the two diamond earrings that Eric bought her.

"What are you doing, girl?" Eric surprisingly asked.

"I wanted to be here for my man, is that a crime?" Rose said, laying on the bed holding the small brown teddy she had bought for Eric.

"Where's Braheem?"

"He came by earlier, and I told him not to tell you that I was in here, that I wanted to cheer you up. So he left so I could surprise you."

"Girl, you are too much," Eric said, finally showing his trademark smile that had been hidden all day.

"Not too much for my man, so are you gonna keep asking questions or come join me and teddy?"

Walking over to his bed, Rose began to slowly undress Eric. "Don't say anything," she said. "You just let me handle everything."

Eric didn't say a word.

Once Eric was totally undressed, Rose laid him down on the large king size bed. "The other night you showed me everything. Now tonight I want to show you what I've learned," she said as she began kissing him around his chest. "I'm new at this so don't get mad if I mess up," she said, easing her tongue towards his rock hard dick. "No teeth, right," Rose said, looking at Eric with her sexy eyes. Eric shook his head yeah. "Joyce told me that," she said smiling.

Grabbing Eric's dick with her hand, she began licking all around its tender and sensitive head. She then gently grabbed both his nuts with her other hand and slowly massaged each of them as she continued to lick around the head of his dick. As Eric laid quiet with both eyes closed, Rose began to devour his large dick in her mouth. As she went up and down with a slow smooth motion, Eric couldn't control the orgasm that was fastly approaching.

"Rose, come here," Eric yelled out. "Come here," he begged in excitement. I'm about to come."

"Not yet, I'm not ready," she said as she continued to massage his nuts and suck every bit of him like a movie porn star.

"Oh, oh, ahhhh," Eric yelled out as he uncontrollably bust off. But without a pause, Rose calmly held onto Eric's dick and swallowed every single drop making sure nothing got unused and nothing got wasted.

"Did I do it right?" she said smiling, "huh, was I okay?"

"Perfect," Eric said shaking his head in disbelief.

"Okay, I'll let you rest for a few. Then it's time for part two," Rose said.

"What have I created?" Eric said smiling from head to toe.

"A monster, that's what you created. A monster," Rose said, laying on his chest. For the remainder of the night, Rose took

Eric's mind away from all that had been going on, as they both enjoyed each other's love and affection.

Chapter Twenty

Thursday afternoon, a few days later ...

Rosemont Cemetary in Philadelphia, Pa. was packed with family and friends all paying their last respects and saying their final goodbyes to Mike.

The sky was a dark grey on this mournful morning as the large group of people all stood around the shiny red coffin that was slowly entering the earth. Eric and Rose stood up front together, tearfully watching Mike's final exit from this cold world. Braheem and Larry both stood on the sides of Mike's mother, holding her from fainting and losing control. As she watched her oldest child leave this world, she screamed, "Oh, God, why my baby? Why Mikey?" She fell to her knees in a pain that only a mother who had ever lost a child would know. Joyce cried as she and her son Ryan threw flowers at the slow moving casket. Almost half of the people from West Park Housing Projects where Mike grew up were there to say their final farewells.

Unable to take it any longer, Eric walked away and Rose quickly followed after him.

"Baby, you all right?" she said, putting her arms around Eric.

"No, I'm not all right, Rose. My best friend is dead and I'm never going to see him again, never," Eric said as his tears started running down his face.

"I'm sorry, Eric. I know how much you loved Mike, but still you must stay focused. Mike's depending on you," Rose said looking into his watery eyes.

"Depending on me for what? He's dead."

"He's gone, but in you, his spirit can still live on."

"What are you talking about Rose?"

"I'm talking about the daycares he wanted so badly for the kids, and his family who depended on his financial help. Mike is still counting on you to be there. To be there for those who still have a chance and to make a difference in someone else's life. Like you did his."

Eric said nothing as he grabbed Rose into his arms and they both cried together. "I'm gonna miss him, Rose," Eric sadly said.

"I know, baby, but everything will be all right," Rose said.

Later that night in Eric's apartment ...

Rose sat on his bed while Eric was inside another room.

"Come here, Rose," Eric said calling her to the room he was in. "Come here for one second," he said.

Rose walked into the room where Eric was and saw him standing on top of a chair.

"What are you doing?" she asked, standing in the door-way.

"Come here. Come closer," Eric said.

Rose walked up to him. "What, baby?" she said.

"I have something to show you, something you need to know."

"What?" she said, wondering what it could be.

Taking off a piece of the drop ceiling, Eric pulled out a large brown leather carrying bag. "Here, hold this," he said.

Reaching up into the ceiling again, he pulled out another large brown leather bag and passed it to Rose. Rose sat them both on the floor without looking inside either.

"Hold up, it's two more," Eric said passing the last two, another brown bag and a white bag. Stepping down off the chair, Eric took a seat.

"What is it?" Rose curiously asked.

Eric opened up a brown bag and dumped everything out on the floor. Stacks of hundred dollar bills laid bundled all together.

"Eric, how much is that?" she asked.

"Five hundred thousand dollars. Each brown bag has $500,000 in them."

"That's two million dollars, Eric. You keep two million dollars in your ceiling?"

"I have a bank account too, but I can't deposit two million bucks in it," Eric said, putting the money back inside the bag.

"That's a lot of money to have just sitting around, Eric."

"I know. I wanted you to know where I had it, just in case."

"Why?"

"Because no one knows and if anything ever happened to me, you would know where all my money was. Braheem don't even know."

"Why me? Why?"

"Because I love you and I know how much you love me."

Picking up the white bag, Eric passed it to Rose.

"What's this?" she said.

"Open it up. There's something in the bottom of the bag."

"What?" Rose said.

"Check and find out," Eric smiling said.

Rose reached into the bag, filing through all the money. She felt something hard inside the bag. Pulling out the small box that was shaped like a rose, a tear rolled down from her eye. "Eric, what's this?" she said shaking nervously.

"Look and see," Eric said with an exciting look on his face.

Opening up the small red rose shaped box, Rose's eyes lit up from what she was seeing. A two carat, rose-colored diamond ring, laced in an 18 carat gold setting, instantly lit up the room.

"Eric! Oh, my God, Eric," Rose said shaking and crying at the same time.

Getting on his knees, he grabbed Rose's shaking hand. Taking the ring out of the box, he placed it on her left finger.

"Will you be my rose forever?" he said, looking up at her beautiful face.

"Yes, Eric, yes, Yes, I would love to be your wife," she said falling to her knees and embracing Eric with a long passionate kiss.

"Here," Eric said, passing her the white bag that was laying next to them on the floor.

"What's this for?"

"It's for us and your family."

"What!" Rose said. "What do you mean?"

"I want you to buy me and you a house and I want you to buy your mother a house too and move her from the projects away from west Philly. That's $500,000 dollars. With that you should be able to do everything."

"Eric, I can't. This is too much money," Rose said.

"Nothing is too much for the woman that's going to be my wife, that's going to be Mrs. Eric Spencer. All my life I waited for you, Rose, and now that I have you, I will never let you go.

If I had the world I would give you half," Eric said.

"I don't believe this," Rose said crying.

"When Mike died last week I realized how short life really was. How Mike died with no wife or kids to be remembered by. Nothing! I thought about my life and how I still could make a change, a difference. Mike's death is the beginning of my new life. And it is you, Rose, that I want to share my new life with. Could you give me the rest of your life, Rose? Could you?" Eric asked looking deep into her dark brown beautiful eyes.

"Yes, Eric, yes, I can. I will give you the rest of my life," Rose said as she continued to cry and stare at the large diamond ring that was on her trembling hand.

Friday afternoon at the post office...

"I am so happy for y'all," Joyce said crying.

"Thank you, Joyce," Rose said showing her the precious diamond stone on her finger.

"He needs someone like you, somebody strong," Joyce said.

"We need each other. What was the three of y'all all talking about at the funeral?" Rose curiously asked.

"Nothing really. He just wants me and Braheem to do him a big favor. Something real personal, that's all."

"He looked so serious when he was talking to y'all."

"He was. He's counting on us to do something for him, but we told him not to worry, that it would get done."

"Joyce, thank you."

"For what, Rose?"

"Thank you for helping to bring Eric into my life. You said that he was special."

"You're welcome, Rose, but you brought Eric into your own life. I can bring him to your house, but only you can open up the door." Joyce said.

"Thank you. I hope that whatever you and Braheem are supposed to do, it gets done 'cause lately he's been so sad."

"It will, when the time is right," Joyce said. "When the time is right."

Friday night at the Platinum Club...

The club was packed as Eric and Braheem sat at the table drinking a bottle of Moet. Beautiful women were walking all around in their tight platinum outfits.

"Do you need anything?" a gorgeous dark woman walked up and asked Eric and Braheem.

"Yes, can you bring us a bottle of Crystal, please." Eric said smiling, showing off his perfect white teeth.

"I'll be right back," the woman said, walking away and into the crowd.

"Did you call Larry and hook that up?" Eric asked.

"Yeah, everything is ready. Everything," Braheem said shaking his head.

"Do you still want to do it?" Eric asked.

"Yeah. It's for Mike. It has to be done," Braheem said admiring all the gorgeous women walking back and forth.

"Do you think she will come?" Braheem asked, looking around the club.

"She will. She's the type that can just smell money."

Walking back up with a bottle of Crystal in her hands, both Eric and Braheem were shocked to see that it was Bunny who had returned instead of the other girl.

"Here's your bottle of Crystal," she said smiling, looking

irresistible in her tight platinum outfit. "Three hundred and fifty dollars. I know y'all ballers can handle that," she said smiling.

Pulling out a large stack of folded hundred dollar bills, Eric passed four of them to Bunny. "Keep the change pretty."

"Can you join us with your fine ass self?" Braheem said.

"I can't just sit around without getting paid, my unc..., I mean my boss will kill me," she said.

"Who said you wouldn't be getting paid? Everything comes with a price," Eric said, putting a large stack of money on top of the table.

With a big smile on her face, Bunny quickly sat down.

"What happened to the other girl?" Braheem asked.

"Oh, she was sent to another table so y'all are stuck with me now," Bunny smiled.

"What's your name, pretty?" Eric asked.

"Bunny," she said in the sweetest and sexiest voice.

"Are you allowed to drink?" Eric said pouring the Crystal into his glass.

"Not on the job," Bunny said, winking her eye.

"What about off the job?" Braheem said.

"Off the job I can do anything I want. For the right price."

"What's the right price?" Eric asked, spreading the money out on the table.

"For you?" Bunny said looking at Eric.

"No, for us?" Eric said looking at Braheem.

"Oh, y'all on some kinky shit, huh?"

"How much," Braheem said.

"A gee apiece. Can y'all handle that?"

Taking ten of the bills from off the table, Eric handed them to Bunny. "Here go, half now, pretty. You ain't saying nothing," Eric said.

"What time you get off?" Braheem asked.

"Now, if y'all are ready to leave," Bunny said, putting the money in her bra.

"Meet us in the parking lot. We'll be in the green BMW."

"It's a few green BMWs in the parking lot," Bunny said standing up.

"The convertible," Braheem said, dangling his keys in the air.

"I'll meet y'all in about 15 minutes. I got to go change and let my unc…, boss know that I'm leaving," Bunny said, walking upstairs to the private rooms in the back.

"We'll be waiting," Eric said as he and Braheem got up from the table and walked out of the club.

Walking upstairs, Bunny ran into Heaven coming from out of a private room.

"Bunny, Bunny, what's up, girl?" Heaven said holding a large stack of bills in her hand.

"I'm about to get paid, girl, that's what's up," Bunny smilingly said.

"What's up, you found you another trick?"

"Yup, two of them," Bunny smiled.

"You go, girl. You need to show me how to pull 'em like you been doing?"

"It's a secret," Bunny said. "Where are you about to go?"

"Your uncle is waiting for me. You know how he gets if he don't get his daily blow job."

"Is he still upset about Rose leaving?"

"Yeah, he makes me dress up in her outfits and suck his dick. He's crazy about Rose. She's all he talks about. Your uncle really wanted her."

"I know. He thinks she looked like his wife who died."

"So that's what it is. Why he would always be glaring at

her all the time."

"Yeah, that and him just being a horny old man," Bunny said laughing. "She knew my uncle liked her. I think she thought that she was too good for him."

"But you know Extacy didn't mess with anybody. All she did was dance and get her money and leave."

"Fuck Extacy! She's a ho, just like every other bitch that works here. She can kiss my white ass. I ain't like her anyway," Bunny said. "Anyway, Heaven, I gots to go. I have two gees waiting for me. I'll see you tomorrow."

"Two geez!"

"That's right. And if they are ballers like that for real, then I'll have two more vicks for my brothers to meet," Bunny smilingly said.

"I'll see you later, Bunny. Let me go see your uncle before he starts trippin'," Heaven said walking towards his private office.

"Okay, Rose," Bunny sarcastically said walking into a dressing room laughing.

Twenty minutes later, Bunny walked out the side door. Seeing Eric and Braheem inside the convertible green BMW with the top down playing **Biggie Small's** *More Money, More Problems,* Bunny walked over and got inside the car.

"Oh, this is my shit. Too bad **Big** and **Tupac** ain't here no more," she said, sitting in the back seat as she pulled out a joint and lit it up.

"What's up? Where we going now?" Bunny said, laying back enjoying the loud music.

"To the hotel," Braheem said.

"Which one?"

"The Sheraton Hotel in Center City," Eric said smiling.

"Okay, y'all ain't playing I see. Y'all ballers for real," Bunny smiled.

"It's only money," Braheem said driving out of the parking lot.

"Unless you want to put a few more hundred in your pocket and we all swing over my man's crib," Eric said.

"Ain't no need in wasting good American presidents, huh?" Bunny said smiling. "Where is it?"

"It's in southwest Philly."

"Oh, it's not too far from here," Bunny said, stretching out on the back seat.

"About 15, 20 minutes," Eric said.

"Okay, cool. Do y'all smoke?" she said, passing the jay around.

"No, we just get money," Braheem said.

"Oh, that's good. My last friend was a cold-blooded junkie with his fake balling ass."

"What was his name? We might know him," Eric said.

"L, Larry, or some shit like that. He drives a silver Mercedes Benz C230, always frontin' with his coke snorting black ass. I know one thing for sure, he won't have much money for long with it all going down his nose," Bunny said grooving to the music.

"Fuck him. You're with some real ballers now," Braheem said, looking at Eric who couldn't believe what he had just heard about Larry.

Chapter Twenty-One

Pulling into the driveway on a small quiet street, Braheem parked and they all got out of the car.

"When will I get the rest of my money?" Bunny asked.

"Once you finish, you'll get everything that's coming to you, that's my word," Eric said smiling.

"Okay," Bunny said. "Y'all won't be disappointed."

"Promise?" Braheem said, walking inside the apartment.

"Bunny always satisfies," she said following them inside and closing the door behind her. "Cute," she said, looking around at the well-furnished apartment.

"Do y'all mind if I use your bathroom?" Bunny politely asked.

"No, it's right there," Braheem said pointing to a door.

"I'll be back in one minute," Bunny said walking into the bathroom and closing the door.

Bunny sat on the toilet and opened up her small black coach purse. Taking out a small bag of powder cocaine and a straw, she began snorting it in her nose. "Umm," she said, "now I'm gonna go fuck both of their brains out," she said enjoying the instant rush.

Standing up, fixing her hair in the mirror, she then took off

187

all of her clothes. "This will fuck them up," she said, closing up her purse with her drugs safely back inside.

Eric and Braheem were sitting on the sofa waiting for Bunny to come out. When Bunny walked out of the bathroom, they both were shocked to see her butt ass naked.

"Oh, shit. Damn!" Braheem said, staring at her gorgeous body. Right over her hairy pussy, a small tattoo said, "Welcome to Fantasy." In her sexiest walk, she moved closer. Her measurements were 38-26-38 and Bunny knew exactly what she was working with.

"Damn, baby, you got a body like a black girl," Braheem said as he felt on her big juicy titties.

"I fuck like a black girl, too," Bunny said, pulling down Braheem's pants.

"No, not right here," Eric said. "The bedroom, it's better."

"Okay, whatever y'all want. It's y'all money. I'm just the Bunny," she said, smiling, as she followed them into a back room.

Entering the bedroom, only a large king size bed, a lamp and a telephone were inside.

"Okay, who's first?" Bunny said, laying on the bed. "Or do y'all both want it at the same time?"

"No, one at a time," Braheem said, taking off all of his clothes.

"Do you play sex games?" Eric asked.

"As long as y'all are paying, Bunny is playing," she said, with her legs wide open.

"We're into sex games," Eric said.

"Like what?"

"We got two masks that we use."

"For what?"

"We cut off the lights, go inside the closet, right here, and one at a time we each come out and fuck you."

"Oh, y'all are on some real kinky shit. Y'all two freaks," she said smiling.

"If you can guess who's the one fucking you, we will give you a hundred dollars every time you're right."

"Okay, I'm ready," Bunny said, laying back. "Y'all never told me your names."

"I'm Jessy," Eric said.

"And I'm James." Braheem said smiling.

Eric then took off all of his clothes. "I'll cut off the light so you can't see. No cheating," he said.

"I'm ready. Let's go," Bunny said smiling. "Y'all are some freaks. But that's what's up," she said. "The freakier the better."

Eric turned off the light and he and Braheem both went into the closet. "Are you ready?" Eric asked, as he and Braheem put on their masks.

"Yeah, I'm ready whenever y'all are," Bunny said, preparing herself for the game.

Opening the door, the first man walked out. Getting on top of Bunny, he quickly put her legs on his shoulders and started fucking her very hard and aggressively. "Oh. Oh. Oh," she screamed. "Ohh, my God, this dick is good. Ohh, your dick is so big," she yelled.

A few moments later, after they had both came, he quickly got up and went back into the closet.

"Who was that?" a voice asked.

"That was Jessy," she said confidently.

"Wrong. You're wrong," a voice said from the closet.

"Oh, shit, come on. I'll get the next one right."

Opening the door again, the next man walked out with a mask on his face. Grabbing Bunny and turning her around, he began fucking her in the ass. "Oh. Oh. Oh," she said, "Ahhh. Ohhh," she yelled, as he pounded her ass from behind. "I'm about to come again. Ohh," she said as they both came together and the man quickly got up and went back into the closet.

"Who was that?" a voice asked once again.

"Both of y'all got big dicks, but I think that was James," she said, laying back on the bed playing with her pussy.

"Wrong again," a voice said.

"What! I was wrong again? Damn," she said, "but I like this game." Bunny smiled.

"One more time. This is your last chance," a voice said.

"You ready?"

"I'm ready. Bring it on. I'll get it right this time."

Opening the door, the next man walked out with his mask on. Laying on the bed, he grabbed Bunny's long blond hair and guided her toward his dick.

"Oh, you want a bow job," she said clutching his dick in her hand.

He shook his head, **"Uh huh."**

Bunny began sucking on his dick as he silently laid on the bed. Up and down she went, making sure she had every inch of him inside of her deep, wet throat. Slowly she gobbled up every drop of him as he quickly came inside her mouth. "Ummm, that tasted good," she said, wiping around her mouth.

Quickly getting up, he went back into the closet.

"Who was that?" a voice said.

"That was Jessy. I know that dick now," she said.

"Wrong," a voice yelled out.

"What! That wasn't Jessy? I was wrong every time," she said in a now upset voice.

"Yup, you were wrong," a voice said.

Both men walked out of the closet and turned on the light.

"I don't believe I was wrong every time," Bunny said.

"You were," Eric said.

"Well, who was first, you Jessy?" she asked looking at both men.

"No, it wasn't me," Eric said smiling.

"Oh, it was you then James?"

"No, it wasn't me either."

"Oh, y'all playing games. Who was it then?" Bunny asked.

"It was me!" Larry said walking from out of the closet with no clothes on, holding a brand new chrome 380 automatic handgun.

"Larry! What's going on? What the fuck is going on?" she said looking at all of them.

"Bitch, fuck you," he said smacking her with his bare hand.

"You fuckin' whore. I thought you loved me. You're just a slut. You set me and my friend up. Your brother killed my man."

Putting their clothes back on, Eric and Braheem didn't say a word.

"Larry, please, they made me do it. My uncle and brother set y'all up."

"You know, I loved you. Just like you said you loved me."

"Forgive me, please," Bunny begged, staring at the tearful Larry. "It was all my brothers and uncle's plan. I swear. We can get them. They're at the club right now. They're the ones who killed your friend. It was my uncle who set it all up. The side door goes right to his office. They're all there now. My uncle and my brothers saw you at his club and told me to go holla at you. They do it all the time," she said nervously shaking. "They saw you inside the club that night, spending money and chasing women, and used me to set you up. Larry, please believe me

191

baby, they made me do it. We can go get them all right now. I
love you, Larry. I do. Please. Please, believe me."

"Shut up bitch! You love money!" Larry said, pulling the
trigger, shooting Bunny twice in the face.

The blood from her face splattered all on Larry's arms and
chest as Bunny's naked body slumped on the bed.

In a bed full of blood, Bunny laid dead. The two bullets that
entered her face instantly killed her. Eric and Braheem remained
silent; neither of them said a word.

"I knew that bitch didn't love me. All she wanted was my
money. You were right, Eric. You said she would fuck anybody
for the right price. You said she would play the game and I
would find out. Fuck this bitch," a disappointed Larry yelled
out.

Standing over her with blood all over himself, Larry shot her
two more times in the chest. "Fuck you, bitch! Fuck you, you
whore!"

"That's enough, Larry. She's dead," Eric said looking at the
horrible scene.

Sitting on the edge of the bed, Larry put his head down
and cried.

"That bitch ain't never loved me. She tried to get me killed."

"Yeah," Braheem said, slowly walking behind Larry as he sat
on the bed crying. "She just wanted your money. That bitch
played you," Braheem said.

Pulling out a long switch blade, Braheem quickly sliced it
across the front of Larry's neck. Dropping the gun on the floor,
Larry quickly put both hands over his bleeding throat, feeling
his breath quickly leaving his body.

With the blood pouring quickly from his open throat, Larry
fell to his knees. Unable to talk, he looked up at Braheem's
face.

"That's for Mike, motha fucka!" Braheem said stepping back.

The blood was quickly running down Larry's chest as he looked over at Eric who was standing in the doorway.

With a tear in his eye, Eric just walked away.

As Larry struggled to stand, his naked body fell over in his own pool of blood. Suddenly, the struggling stopped. Wiping the switchblade off, Braheem placed it inside of Bunny's hand. With his eyes wide open, Larry laid dead, still holding his bloody throat. Walking over to the phone, Braheem picked it up and called the police.

"9-1-1," a female voice answered.

"I'm about to kill this cheating bitch. She pulled a blade out on me," Braheem said.

"Calm down, everything will be okay. Someone is on the way now," the voice said. "Please don't do anything stupid."

"Fuck this whore!" Braheem said, hanging up the phone. With his black gloves on, he placed the telephone next to Larry's dead body and quickly left the room. Walking out the door, Eric was outside waiting. Getting inside the car, they drove off.

"Did you take care of that?" Eric said, driving away from Larry's apartment.

"Yup, it's all taken care of," Braheem said.

When the police arrived at Larry's apartment, the front door was unlocked. When they walked inside, they discovered the two dead bodies laying a few feet away from each other. Homicide detectives soon arrived and closed off the murder scene. From the look of the crime, it appeared to look like a violent domestic abuse between two lovers who eventually killed one another, a scene that the lead homicide investigator on the case had seen many times. Still, he would have to do his job and make sure that was the case here as well.

Chapter Twenty-Two

Forty-five minutes later ...

Inside the Platinum Club parking lot, Eric and Braheem sat in the car, waiting, just a few feet from the side exit door.

"You ready?" Eric asked Braheem who had a ski mask in his hand.

"I'm ready, E. Let's do this," he said.

Standing by the side door where the strippers would come out, Eric and Braheem both waited.

"This is the door that goes up to his office," Eric said.

Pulling out a small screwdriver, Eric quickly picked the door's lock. Taking the ski mask from his back pocket, he put it on and so did Braheem. Walking inside, no one was in the small hallway as they both pulled out two 9 mm handguns.

On one side of the hall, a sign on a door said "Dancers Only." On the other side, wooden steps went up. They both took the stairs.

Reaching the top of the stairs, a sign on a door said, "Please, do not enter. Management only."

Peeping through a small glass window, Eric could see four men talking. One was sitting behind a desk with stacks of money in front of him, while the other three men all stood around. Closely, Eric listened.

"Where's Bunny, Mario," Mr. Perotta said.

"She hasn't called yet. She's still out, Uncle P.," Mario said.

"Did you and Vinny find out where that mooley lives?" he said.

"No, Uncle P, not yet," Vinny answered.

"Marty drove us around all day trying to find that nigger," Mario said.

"Don't worry, boss, we will find him and do what we did to his friend," Marty said, rubbing down his long black ponytail.

"I want his ass dead. We can't take no chances," Mr. Perotta said. "That nigger can cause a lot of problems for us."

"We will take care of him, Unc, I promise," Vinny said.

With their masks on and 9 mm's gripped in both their hands, at the same time Eric and Braheem kicked open the door and rushed in, catching everyone by surprise.

"Everybody put your hands up," Eric yelled, pointing his gun.

"Put your fuckin' hands up now," Braheem said.

"Y'all three, get against the wall," Eric said to the men who were standing all with scared looks on their faces.

Vinny, Mario and Marty all walked and faced the wall.

"Take the money," Mr. Perotta said. "You can have the money. It's all yours, here, two million dollars, every penny the club made this week," Mr. Perotta said putting it all inside of a briefcase.

Braheem walked over and grabbed the briefcase from Mr. Perotta's hand.

"You have the money now. Can you leave? We don't want no problems," Mr. Perotta said, slowly easing open a secret drawer in his desk.

"This is not about money," Eric said.

"What is it about?"

"It's about revenge, revenge for killing my best friend," Eric said as he and Braheem began shooting all three me who faced the wall.

All three of their bodies quickly fell to the ground, each with life ending results.

Turning around, Eric faced Mr. Perotta. "You're behind everything," he said. "You're the reason my friend is dead."

With his hand now gripped on a 38 revolver under his desk, Mr. Perotta pulled the trigger, hitting Eric twice in the stomach.

Braheem suddenly began firing as Mr. Perotta ducked under his desk and began shooting out of control in fear for his life.

A stumbling Eric managed to make it out the door. With the briefcase in his hand, Braheem grabbed Eric, helping him down the steps. After getting Eric into his waiting car, Braheem got in and quickly drove off.

"Eric, hold on. Hold on, cuz, I'm a get you to a hospital," Braheem said.

"Hurry up, Braheem, hurry up," Eric said, feeling the burn in his stomach intensify.

"The hospital is not too far, just hold on, Eric, we're almost there," Braheem said driving through every red light. "Hold on. You just be strong, Eric."

"Hurry up," Eric said with his hands over his bloody shirt holding his stomach.

"I got to drop you off Eric. I got to get rid of these guns and ski masks," Braheem said.

"I'll be okay, just hurry up, Braheem, and get to the hospital."

"Few more blocks, just hold on, Eric, we'll be there in one minute."

"If I don't make it, tell Rose I love her," Eric said breathing heavily.

"You're going to tell Rose that you love her, hold on," Braheem said, as he turned down the corner to the University of Pennsylvania Hospital's emergency room. "You're gonna tell her, now just hold on a little bit longer."

Pulling the car onto the curb, Braheem began hollering.

"Somebody, help, a man has been shot," he yelled. "Please, somebody call a doctor," he said helping Eric out of the car.

Two doctors who were talking outside quickly rushed to Eric's aid.

"He's been shot," Braheem said.

"Okay, son, we got him. We got him now," one of the men said holding Eric up.

Braheem ran back to his car once Eric was inside the hospital. He sped off disappearing into the night.

Chapter Twenty-Three

University of Pennsylvania Hospital, one week later ...

Outside Eric's room, Braheem was talking to a doctor. "Doc, why ain't he waking up?" Braheem tearfully asked.

"He's in a coma. His condition is very bad. The gunshot wounds caused serious damage to his kidney and liver. All we can do now is wait," the doctor said, walking away.

Inside, Rose and Joyce sat crying beside Eric's bed. "Baby, it's me. It's me, Rose," she said holding his hand. With his eyes closed and tubes inside of his body, the two women could do nothing but cry and continue to wait.

"Please, God, don't take Eric away. Please, not him *and* Mike. Please," Joyce cried.

"Honey, you promised me that you would be there. Don't back out now," Rose tearfully said. "You got people out here who needs you, who love you."

But all their cries and prayers were useless. Eric's life was now in God's hands only.

Two doctors walked into the room interrupting the emotional moment.

"I'm sorry ladies, but visiting is now over. We have a few more tests to run. Could y'all please leave the room?" the short doctor with the thick glasses said, holding a large pad in his hands.

"Visiting will begin again tomorrow at noon," the older grey-haired doctor said, replacing a plastic tube from Eric's mouth.

"Doc, will everything be okay?" Rose asked, as she and Joyce walked to the door.

"It's all up to Eric now. We've done all we could do. We have one of the best medical staffs in the country, but nothing, not even the million dollar equipment in this hospital can help more than the determination to live. All I can tell y'all now is to pray. Pray that Eric has that determination."

Knowing it was all up to Eric now, tearfully, both women walked out the door.

Inside Eric's Infiniti, Braheem, Rose and Joyce were talking. "Everything will be okay, Rose. Eric is strong," Braheem said, driving down Spruce Street in west Philadelphia.

"It's been one whole week. He hasn't even moved," Rose said crying.

"The doc said the body is in some type of shock, that it tries to heal itself," Joyce said, crying too.

"Eric lost a lot of blood, but he's a warrior," Braheem said.

"I got to do something. I just can't sit back and do nothing," Rose said.

"But it's nothing you could do, neither of us. You heard what the doctor said, it's all up to Eric now," Joyce said.

"All we can do now is be there for him, and like the doctor said, 'pray,'" Braheem said.

"Rose, Eric will come through. I know he will, and he will be so proud of the things you have done once he finds out. Once he comes back to us, he will be so proud of you," Joyce said.

"I need him back, or it will be nothing without him. It would all be meaningless. We were supposed to enjoy all of it together. I have so much to tell him, things he needs to know. He can't leave me now." Rose said. "He can't leave me now," Rose began crying.

"Everything will be okay, Rose, keep your head up," Braheem said. "And just pray and don't give up."

Controlling his tears, Braheem continued to drive as both women cried the whole ride back home.

Sitting on her bed that night, Rose wrote a poem.

Who Made You God?

"I'm drifting without you here,

I'm all alone. Afraid. I'm a lost child in a lost world with no direction.

I tried to run from love, instead I ran into you.

How could you kidnap my heart and hold it forever?

Who told you to love me? Who sent you here? Where did you come from?

I'm a rose, but you've become my sun and rain.

Making it so hard to grow without you. Why? Who gave you this magical power to come into people's lives and love them?

And confuse them. I was focused, but my vision soon became foggy,

Making me lose sight of what I was doing and where I was going.

This can't be a part of the plan. This can't be the way it was supposed to be. Or can it? I pray that it's not.

Who said you could steal my heart, I ask you? Please tell me.

You're nothing but a thief. A thief of love. A thief who plots on confused minds.

*You take what you want, without asking. Who do you think
you are?*
  Tell me, who made you God?"
  Laying back on her bed, Rose grabbed her white teddy bear
and began crying, hoping that things would be better tomor-
row and Eric would come back to her.
  Later that night, Joyce and Braheem sat on her steps talk-
ing.
  "Are we still going to do that?" Joyce asked.
  "Yeah, but we got to wait for Eric."
  "I'm afraid, Braheem, I'm really scared. Eric is like my
brother. I can't imagine him not being here," Joyce tearfully
said.
  "I'm scared too, but Eric needs me and you to be strong.
He's counting on us."
  "I know. I know, but it's so hard seeing him in that hospi-
tal like that."
  "All we can do, Joyce, is wait."
  "First Mike, then Larry, now this. I can't take no more,"
Joyce said.
  "You can't stress yourself, things happened for a reason,
and sometimes things happen to good people. And sometimes,
bad people get what they deserve."
  "But, Eric is a good man. He don't deserve to be all shot up
like that."
  "None of us deserves this life we live, Joyce. I ask God sometimes, why does He take us through so much. Why do people
like us have to go through so much to survive? Why is it so
hard for us? Will we ever see the light at the end of the tunnel?
Or will the tunnel stay dark forever?" Braheem said, looking
deep into Joyce's eyes. "Here," Braheem said, passing Joyce a
small white card.

"Put this up until we need it," he said, still staring into her eyes.

"Why are you looking at me like that, Braheem?"

"Because I think you're beautiful," Braheem said.

"What! You never told me this before," Joyce blushingly said.

"I'm telling you now," Braheem said, as he reached over and the two of them began kissing passionately. "I'll talk to you later," Braheem said as he walked away leaving Joyce sitting on the step wanting more.

Getting back inside of Eric's Infinity, Braheem drove off.

Taking out a picture from her jacket of herself, Mike and Eric when they were all young kids living in the projects, Joyce could only reminisce about the good old days, and the wonderful kiss she just got from Braheem.

Two days later...

The five large Italian men all stood around as Mr. Perotta was talking. "They said they was friends of the kid that was killed. I want these men tracked down and killed. I want their family dead, their friends and anybody else who's associated with these punks."

"Sir, we've been looking. We been searching all throughout southwest Philly, like you asked. Something will come up soon. Me and my boys will keep looking, Mr. Perotta," one of the men said.

"These fuckin' punks killed my two nephews and my friend and robbed me of two million dollars. Somebody must know something."

"The police haven't got a clue. All they know is that I was robbed and people were killed by two masked men. This shit must get handled soon. My patience is running thin."

"Sir, we checked all the streets in southwest. We even checked the clubs. The pool halls. No one seems to know anything," another one of the guys said, hitting his palm.

Sitting in his chair, Mr. Perotta looked at the two bullet holes in his desk.

"I think I shot him!" he said. "Yeah, I think I shot him."

"What, sir?" a man asked.

"I think I shot him at least once when I fired my gun."

"You never told us this. Why you never mentioned it before?"

"I wasn't sure, but I think so. I want y'all to check every damn hospital in the city. Find out if a man was shot last week and a half ago."

"That will be hard, sir," a man said.

"I don't care how hard it is, or how long it takes. Get it done."

"My nephews are dead and my friend is dead, too, and on top of all that, my niece was killed by some fuckin' fatal attraction. This has been the worst week of my godamn life. Four people are dead and two million dollars is gone," Mr. Perotta said, standing up. "Here, here's my card, you call me when you find out something. I'll be at home," he said, walking out the door. "My cell phone number is on the card. You come with me," he said, pointing to one of the large men who stood around.

Sunday night, three days later...

Inside the University of Pennsylvania Hospital, Eric's mother had just left as Rose sat alone by Eric's bed.

"Are you okay?" a nurse asked, peeping in the door.

"Yes, I'm fine, thank you," Rose said, as the nurse smiled and walked away.

Suddenly, Eric's body began trembling.

"Eric! Eric, it's me. It's me, Rose, baby. Oh, my God! Eric."

Again his body shook as Rose grabbed is hand and held tightly.

"Eric, baby, wake up. It's me. Do you hear me?" she said.

After the scariest week of Rose's life, both Eric's eyes finally opened.

"Eric! Eric! It's me! Me, Rose! Can you understand?" she said, looking into his confused looking eyes. "Please, Eric, say something. Please. It's me, Rose," she cried. "Eric! Can you hear me? Say something, anything."

"I love you, Rose," he finally said in a low sickly voice.

"Oh, Eric," she said, hugging him. "You're gonna be all right. Thank you, God. Eric, you scared me. I'm going to go get the doctor. Wait one minute, baby," Rose said, standing up.

"No, no, don't go nowhere, not yet," Eric said.

Rose sat back down by his side.

"I see you're wearing your ring," Eric said, looking at her hand.

"Yes, I'll never take it off. I love you, Eric."

"I love you too. Where's Braheem?"

"Him and Joyce are on their way over here. They will be here soon."

"Good. I got to talk to both of them. It's very important."

"Eric, I have some good news to tell you, baby."

"What? What do you got to tell me beautiful?"

"I bought us a house and I moved my family into a house too."

"You did?"

"Yes, a few days ago. I bought my mom a nice small house in northeast Philadelphia. And I got me and you a townhouse out Pennrose Avenue. All of your money is put up in a safe I bought you. Everything is all taken care of," Rose tearfully smiled.

"I knew I could count on you, baby," Eric said in a low voice.

"That's not all. I met with your lawyer last week. We purchased the building you wanted. It's all paid for. Your lawyer is taking care of all the necessary paperwork for the licensing of the daycare, before the renovation on the building starts."

"Rose, thank you so much, baby."

"I love you, and I want to spend the rest of my life with you," Rose said.

"You will. I'll never leave you again," I promise.

"You better not. Oh, I almost forgot. Braheem gave me a briefcase. I put it up and didn't open it yet. It's inside of the safe too."

Shaking his head, a smile appeared on Eric's face.

A few moments later...

Joyce and Braheem walked into the room

"Eric! Eric! You're okay," Joyce said walking over to him and hugging him.

"Eric, you scared us, man," Braheem said, kneeling down by the bed.

"Did y'all do that?" Eric asked.

"No, not yet. We waited for you," Joyce said wiping her tears.

"Eric, you better not ever frighten us like this again," Rose said.

Eric then tried to sit up on his bed.

"Are you okay, baby?" Rose said, helping him sit up.

"I'm fine. Joyce, you and Braheem can go do that now. I'll see y'all both later. I got to talk to Rose alone."

"Okay, Eric, we'll be back soon after we take care of everything. It will be done today, Eric, don't worry about a thing," Joyce said.

"What are y'all talking about?" Rose said.

"It's nothing. Now come here and let me taste those soft lips."

"Yeah, okay, you and your surprises," Rose said, kissing Eric.

Standing up, Joyce and Braheem rushed out of the room leaving Eric and Rose alone.

"Rose, I'm so sorry, baby, for all that I've been taking you through."

"Eric, all of this is scaring me, but I love you."

"And I love you. Rose, thank you for everything, and thank you so much for getting the building for the daycare."

"What are you going to call it?"

"I had something in mind."

"What? Tell me!" Rose said.

"Roses among thorns. I believe every child in the ghetto is like a rose, a rose that's trying to escape all of the thorns that keep them down. The drugs, poverty, crime, AIDs, rape, guns and deaths. These are all thorns. And the young children of the ghettos are like roses. See, no matter how hard a thorn sticks us and hurts us, a rose will still grow. Nothing can ever stop a rose from growing. That's what I want to call my daycares. Roses among thorns ... so children can know, they still have a chance, that they still can grow."

"Eric, that is so beautiful," Rose said crying. "Eric, I need to ask you something. Something that's very important to me."

"What? You can ask me anything, go ahead."

"Can I have you? Can you be all of mine? And no one else's?"

"Rose, what are you talking about? You got me. I am all of yours."

"No, Eric, I don't have you, she does."

"Who? What are you talking about?"

"The game! Eric, can you leave her alone, for me, could I be the only woman in your life?"

"Rose ..."

"Eric, please answer me. Eric, can you walk away from this deadly game?"

"Yes, Rose, for you, beautiful, yes, I'm done."

"Thank you, Eric, thank you, baby. Thank you so much," she said crying. "I'll be right back. I have to go do something. I have to go somewhere," Rose said, standing up smiling. "I have to do something that's very important!"

"Where? Where are you going?"

"I'll be back soon," she said running out of the room.

Chapter Twenty-Four

That night ...

Mr. Perotta was relaxing in his Jacuzzi, smoking on a custom cigar, when his cell phone rang.

"Hello," he said, answering his cell phone.

"Hi, Mr. Perotta, it's me, Rose."

"Who's this?"

"It's me, Rose."

"Rose! So you finally decided to call me, huh?"

"Yes, I was thinking about you. I'm so sorry about Bunny."

"Thank you, Rose. So what can I do for you, beautiful?"

"I thought about your offer. I wanted to know if it was still available."

"Yes, it's still available for you, my sweet Rose."

"Well, I would like to see you. I heard so many big things about you."

"Oh, yeah? What did you hear?"

"All the girls at the club talk about you, big daddy. I wanted to find out on my own."

"Well, you can meet me at my office at the club."

"No. No, not the club. I don't want anybody knowing about our business. You know, I'm very private. That's why I kept telling you no before."

"Right now is really a bad time, Rose. So much has been going on. It's really a bad time. Could we do this another day, sweetie?"

"That's why I called you, so I could help ease some of the pain I know you're going through. I just wanted to be there for you."

"Okay, Rose. I'll be there for you, my darling. You know I've been wanting you for a long time."

"I know and now you can finally have me. I'll be in room 103 at the Love Nest Hotel on 18th Street."

"I'm on my way. Room 103, right?" Mr. Perotta said getting out of the Jacuzzi.

"Right. You can just walk in, I'm already in bed waiting for you."

"I'm on my way. I'll be there in 40 minutes," Mr. Perotta said, quickly hanging up the phone.

"I knew she would be calling me soon," Mr. Perotta said to himself, as he grabbed a nearby towel and started drying off his body.

Forty-five minutes later ...

Mr. Perotta and one of his bodyguards pulled into the Love Nest Hotel's entrance and parked his black Lincoln Towncar.

"Wait right here. I'll be about an hour," Mr. Perotta said, getting out of the car and walking into the hotel.

Walking down the hall, he finally reached room 103 and walked inside. The lights were dimmed, the smell of an exotic perfume filled the room.

"Rose? Rose, it's me. It's me, big daddy, beautiful," Mr. Perotta said.

"I'm in the bedroom," a sweet voice answered.

"Can I cut on the light? It's dark in here. I can hardly see."

"No, I don't like the light. It spoils my mood," she said,

in a sexy voice.

"Okay, whatever you want beautiful. Whatever you like."

Walking into the dark bedroom, Mr. Perotta stopped at the foot of the bed. "Why are you hiding that beautiful face under the covers?"

"I'm cold. Come, make me warm, daddy."

"Okay, daddy is on his way," he said walking up closer.

"First, take off all your clothes. Hurry, hurry. I'm cold daddy."

Taking off all of his clothes, Mr. Perotta got on the bed.

"Can daddy have a kiss first, Rose?"

"First, I want you to taste me. Can you taste me, daddy?"

"Anything for you," he said, going under the covers.

"Oh, Rose, your pussy is so hairy," he said as he began to lick around her clitoris. "Umm, umm, Rose, you taste good, beautiful. I knew you would call."

"Oh, daddy, that feels so good. Oh, I love the way you eat my pussy," she said. "Ohhh, don't stop."

Reaching under her pillow, she slowly grabbed a chrome 9 mm with a silencer attached. "Ohh, daddy, oh, daddy, I'm about to come," she said holding the gun to his head as he continued to eat her pussy.

"Mr. Perotta? Mr. Perotta?" She said.

"Yes, beautiful, yes, what is it?"

"Do you know what this pussy is? Do you?"

"No, tell me. Tell me. What?"

"It's your last meal mothafucka!" she said, pulling the trigger, putting four quick and silent bullets into his forehead instantly killing him.

"That was for Mike," she said, leaving his bleeding body under the covers.

Mr. Perotta's naked body slumped to the bed as his blood

quickly filled the sheets. The woman then got up and went into his pants pockets that were on the floor.

After taking out a large stack of money, she then got dressed in a Muslim woman's veil where only her eyes were showing and walked out of the room and down the empty hall.

Walking out of a back door exit, she quickly got into a waiting car.

"Is everything done, Joyce?"

"Everything is done, Braheem. That guy really was obsessed with Rose."

"Just like Eric said he was," Braheem said driving away.

"What do you want me to do with this?" she said holding Mr. Perrota's white card in her hand.

"Burn it and throw it out the window. We don't need it anymore."

"What about this money?" she said, holding the large stack of hundreds.

"Eric told you that whatever it was, to keep it. It's yours, Joyce."

"Take me back to change my clothes. I want to go back and see Eric."

"Okay," Braheem said, watching Joyce burn the card and throw it out the window.

Driving out of the parking lot, Joyce noticed Mr. Perotta's bodyguard slumped over inside of the car. "Oh, I took care of him while you were inside," Braheem said, as he continued to drive away. "No witnesses, no case."

"Nobody but me and you," Joyce smilingly said.

"Me and you," Braheem nodded.

"Me and you," Joyce said, as she reached over and kissed him on his cheek.

Chapter Twenty-Five

Back at the hospital ...

Eric was sitting up in his bed as a doctor was checking his pulse and condition. "You'll be fine, son, everything is working normally, your liver and kidney both will be okay. For now, you seem to be healing perfectly well."

"Thanks, doc."

"You still will need plenty of rest. You are a very, very lucky young man. Thank God, because things could have been a lot different."

"I will, doc." Eric said, shaking his head in agreement.

"One more thing," the doctor said, walking out the door. "That woman you have, Rose, take care of her. She's a real good woman. She never left your side," he said.

"Thank you. I will," Eric smiled.

"Goodbye, Eric. I'll check back on you in a few hours," the doctor said, walking out the door.

The phone then rang that was on the table next to Eric's bed.

"Hello," he said, picking it up.

"Eric, it's me," Braheem said talking on his cell phone.

"Where's Joyce?"

"She's right here, sitting next to me."

"Was everything done?"

"Yeah, everything is taken care of. Just like you planned it."

"Tell Joyce thank you."

"I will. We'll see you in a few, goodbye," Braheem said, shutting his cell phone.

Once again, Eric smiled as he laid back on his pillow.

Moments later ...

Rose walked back into Eric's room. Taking out a small white envelope from her purse, she passed it to Eric.

"Where did you go? What's this?

"I went home. I had to get this envelope for you."

"What is it?

"Open it and find out. I don't know. What's it say? It's from my father. He told me to only give it to you if you answered the question right."

"What question? What are you talking about?"

"About leaving the game alone and finally walking away."

"Oh, yeah, he did," Eric smilingly said.

"He said he knew you would come through and told me to give it to you once you came to. I've been holding it for almost a week. Open it! Hurry up and open it!"

"Hold up, girl," Eric said, as he began opening up the small white envelope.

Taking out the piece of paper that was inside, Eric opened it and began to read it to himself.

"Welcome to the family, son. You now have all my blessings," it said.

Eric sat back and smiled again.

"What did it say? What did it say?" Rose curiously asked.

"Here," Eric said, passing the piece of paper to Rose.

After reading the piece of paper, Rose smiled and she and

Eric just gave each other a big hug.

"I love you, Eric, I love you so much," Rose said, crying on his shoulder.

"I love you too, Rose," Eric said. "I love you too."

Fan Mail Page

If you have any further questions, comments or concerns,
kindly address your inquires in care of:

Jimmy DaSaint
At

DASAINT ENT
P.O.BOX 97
BALA CYNWYD, PA
19004

www.dasaintentertainment.com
or
dasaintent@gmail.com

DASAINT ENTERTAINMENT ORDER FROM

ORDERING BOOKS

Please visit www.dasaintentertainment.com to place online orders.
You can also fill out this from and sent it to:

DASAINT ENTERTAINMENT
PO BOX 97
BALA CYNWYD, PA 19004

TITLE	PRICE	QTY
BLACK SCARFACE	$15.00	_____
BLACK SCARFACE II	$15.00	_____
YOUNG RICH & DANGEROUS	$15.00	_____
WHAT EVERY WOMAN WANTS	$15.00	_____
THE UNDERWORLD	$15.00	_____
A ROSE AMONG THORNS	$15.00	_____
A ROSE AMONG THORNS II	$15.00	_____
MONEY DESIRES AND REGRETS	$15.00	_____
ON EVERYTHING I LOVE	$15.00	_____
AIN'T NO SUNSHINE	$15.00	_____

Make Checks or Money Orders out to: DASAINT ENTERTAINMENT

NAME:_____

ADDRESS:_____

CITY:_____ STATE:_____ ZIP:_____

TELEPHONE:_____

EMAIL:_____

$3.50 Shipping, plus $1.50 EACH additional book For Shipping and Handling

($4.95 For Expedited Shipping per item)
WE SHIP TO PRISONS!!!

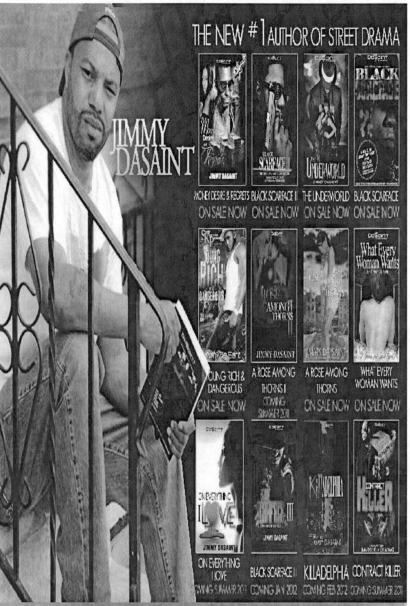

CPSIA information can be obtained at www.ICGtesting.com
Printed in the USA
LVOW10s1558290416

485950LV00018B/508/P